Wᴵʟʟɪᴀᴍ
Sʜᴀᴋᴇsᴘᴇᴀʀᴇ's

# A Mɪᴅsᴜᴍᴍᴇʀ Nɪɢʜᴛ's Dʀᴇᴀᴍ

Love makes fools of us all.

ADAPTED FOR THE SCREEN AND DIRECTED BY MICHAEL HOFFMAN

RUPERT EVERETT

CALISTA FLOCKHART

KEVIN KLINE

MICHELLE PFEIFFER

STANLEY TUCCI

WILLIAM SHAKESPEARE'S

A MIDSUMMER NIGHT'S DREAM

Love makes fools of us all.

HarperEntertainment
*A Division of HarperCollinsPublishers*
http://www.harpercollins.com

Grateful acknowledgment is made to the following for permission to reprint images from copyrighted material:

Luciana Arrighi for production design sketches;

Gabriella Pescucci for costume design sketches;

Private collection/Bridgeman Art Library, London/New York for Etruscan Musicians, copy of a 5th century BC fresco in the Tomb of the Leopard at Tarquinia;

Musee Gustave Moreau, Paris, France/Bulloz/Bridgeman Art Library, London/New York for *The Muses Leave Their Father Apollo to Go Out and Light the World*, 1868, by Gustave Moreau (1826-98);

Boboli Gardens, Florence, Italy/Bridgeman Art Library, London/New York for *The Bacchus Fountain*, c.1560 (marble), by Valerio di Simone Cioli (1529-99);

Manchester City Art Galleries, UK/Bridgeman Art Library, London/New York for *Hylas and the Nymphs*, 1896, by John William Waterhouse (1849-1917);

Musee Gustave Moreau, Paris, France/Peter Willi/Bridgeman Art Library, London/New York for *Jupiter and Semele*, by Gustave Moreau (1826-98);

Private collection for *Vesper*, or *The Evening Star*, 1872, by Edward Burne-Jones.

HarperCollins books may be purchased for educational, business, or sales promotional use. For information please write: Special Markets Department, HarperCollins Publishers Inc., 10 East 53rd Street, New York, NY 10022-5299.

FIRST EDITION

Designed by Jeannette Jacobs

Library of Congress Cataloging-in-Publication Data is available

ISBN 0-06-107356-3

99 00 01 02 10 9 8 7 6 5 4 3 2 1

FOR SAMANTHA FOR THE INSPIRATION

*The world of the film is Tuscany at the turn of the last century. Necklines are high. Parents are rigid. Social convention dictates the fate of the young. Class distinction is a large part of everyday life and to be an aristocrat still means something. The good news: The bustle is on its decline allowing for the meteoric rise of this newfangled creation, the bicycle.*

# INTRODUCTION

*But man is but a patched fool if he will offer to say*
*    what methought I had.*
*The eye of man hath not heard,*
*The ear of man hath not seen, man's hand is not*
*able to taste, his tongue to conceive, nor his heart*
*to report, what my dream was.*

                                                    —Bottom

   A Midsummer Night's Dream relies for its success on the interplay between diverse worlds, diverse perspectives, and the implicit unity that underlies them. It's easier with *Midsummer* to make the jokes work than to express that unity. What common motivation could one hope to find among characters as different as Titania, Queen of the Fairies, and Snout the Tinker?

   I imagined the characters placed side by side along a continuum. At one end I labeled it, "Anything for Love," and at the other, "No Compromise." Nearest "No Compromise" I placed Egeus, whose neurotic legalism makes him willing to threaten his daughter's happiness rather than feel himself diminished by the loss of control. Next to him I put Oberon. Subtler by far, he is happy still to wrangle endlessly in his petty power struggle with Titania rather than take up the olive branch and rescue nature from chaos.

   At the other end of the spectrum I put the mechanicals, and in an even more extreme position, Helena. She shows herself ready to undergo any humiliation for the poorest scrap of Demetrius' affection:

*Use me but as your spaniel; spurn me, strike me*
*Neglect me, lose me; only give me leave*
*Unworthy as I am, to follow you.*

   Ironically, it is Oberon who reaches across the divide to become her champion. The love he cannot provide his fairy consort, he is compelled to provide this poor, befuddled mortal.

   Everyone in the play wants to be loved, but love's attainment for each of them has obstacles imposed from within or without. For the four lovers, the primary obstacles are their own conditioned notions of themselves. If Thomas Mann is right and all the world breaks down into lovers and beloveds, Helena understands herself only as the first. Love does not exist without suffering and humiliation. The lover is always a victim. It is only when her misguided perception is mirrored back to her in the lovesick obsession of the enchanted Lysander and Demetrius that she shows any interest in power or dignity:

*Wherefore was I to this keen*
*    mockery born?*
*When at your hands did I*
*    deserve such scorn?*

   Hermia is very much the "beloved." She understands herself only as the object of affection, of both boys' passionate desire, and of her father's obsessive attachment. In her first meeting with Helena, she reveals a corresponding blind spot. She is unable to empathize. The comfort she offers seems less than truly felt. It is simply a preamble to news of her own happy passion.

Again, in the woods, rather than give herself to Lysander, Hermia tests his love. One senses, even before he deserts her, that she has built a little tower for herself, at least as lonely as the muck in which Helena grovels.

The girls are stuck in preconceived notions of themselves. But *A Midsummer Night's Dream* is Shakespeare's essay on love and transformation. Puck, the great subverter of conditioning, cannot abide such negative stases. Transform they must. Just as Helena is forced to see herself as the beloved, Hermia has to feel the abject pain of the humiliated lover. It is the forest's way of leading them toward a more broad-ranging identity, a fuller realization of who they are.

Puck stands at the very center of the continuum, suspended by the tension between his desire to please Oberon and his fundamental love of chaos. He wants to execute Oberon's desires—wants nothing more than for Oberon to love him—but he cannot, in the moment, help but play, fiddle, upset, manipulate. Always true to his own nature, he intervenes to create the crises that will lead to change.

These issues of conditioning and its subversion led me naturally to the late Victorian setting. In a world dominated by convention, but poised on the verge of a dramatic shift, there seemed no better visual metaphor for the repression of the Self than stiff collars, high necklines, tight corsets, and silly accessories. (And then to lose it all in the dark, elemental night.)

For the fairy world I turned to the symbolist painting of the same period—the dark pagan sensuality of Gustave Moreau, the brooding landscapes of Bocklin laced with hints of unseen ritual, figures and images that spring uninvited from the dark pool of the unconscious. That these images owed a debt to Ovid's *Metamorphoses* seemed right, as it was one of Shakespeare's own sources for the poetic imagery of the play.

Love and dignity, conditioning and subversion, a rich world of images: still the adaptation lacked a center in terms of character. I thought of bookending the play by making it the dream of Theseus, Hipployta, or Helena, but it was Nick Bottom I returned to again as I read and reread the play.

It wasn't Bottom the egotist, the clumsy outspoken braggart, nor Bottom the buffoon. It was Nick Bottom the dreamer, the actor, the pretender—Nick Bottom sitting at a café in a small Italian town dressed in a white suit, trying his best to look like the gentleman. It is only when we learn that it is the only suit he owns, that he has a lousy marriage, that he lives in a dingy flat, that we know he clings to delusions of grandeur because he has no love in his life.

To imagine Bottom's desire for love led to a remarkable opportunity for a real love story between him and the Fairy Queen. Usually this relationship is played for the comedy alone. Titania moons and coos in her enchanted haze. Bottom becomes the Oriental pasha, more concerned with having his ears scratched and his belly filled than engaging her uncensored affection.

But if Bottom actually changed and grew through his experience in the forest, and glimpsed the possibility that he was truly lovable, it might give the film the emotional spine I'd wanted. It would also give Titania dimension. I suddenly saw her as a woman who wanted to love simply, unconditionally, in a way the politics of her relationship with Oberon made impossible. Titania and Bottom's struggle with love and pride, and their simple, if brief, discovery of each other, felt like a gift.

Kevin Kline would be perfect to play this Bottom. The problem was that when he and I had first talked about it, he was to play Oberon—the grandeur, the romance, the power, the language (of course). When I approached him with this amendment to the plan, he resisted.

Only after many conversations did the phone ring late one Sunday night. It was Kevin. He had devised a way that he could play Oberon, Bottom, *and* Theseus. I breathed a sigh of relief. He'd already begun his work. He was Bottom volunteering to play Thisbe, the lion, the wall—everything.

Why *A Midsummer Night's Dream*? For its magic, its innocence, its comedy, its poetry, the untarnished soul of Peter Quince, the mythic power and beauty of Titania—to be part of the four-hundred-year-old pageant that is Shakespeare in performance.

Virginia Woolf once said that were a man to read *Hamlet* each year of his life and make notes on his reading, at the end of his life he would have written his autobiography. Whether or not the same could be said of *Midsummer*, it is a play that, like a magic mirror, enchants us and reflects back to us who we are, and what we know of love.

—Michael Hoffman, Director

*Kevin Kline as Bottom, John Sessions as Philostrate, and director Michael Hoffman discuss the play.*

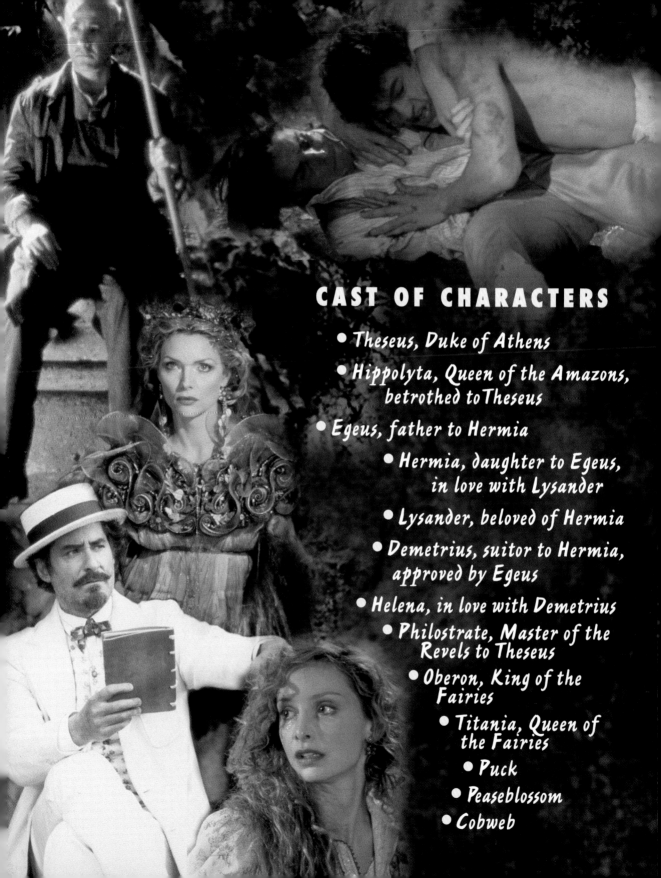

# CAST OF CHARACTERS

- *Theseus, Duke of Athens*
- *Hippolyta, Queen of the Amazons, betrothed to Theseus*
- *Egeus, father to Hermia*
- *Hermia, daughter to Egeus, in love with Lysander*
- *Lysander, beloved of Hermia*
- *Demetrius, suitor to Hermia, approved by Egeus*
- *Helena, in love with Demetrius*
- *Philostrate, Master of the Revels to Theseus*
- *Oberon, King of the Fairies*
- *Titania, Queen of the Fairies*
- *Puck*
- *Peaseblossom*
- *Cobweb*

- Moth
- Mustardseed
- Peter Quince, a carpenter; Prologue in the interlude
- Nick Bottom, a weaver; Pyramus in the interlude
- Francis Flute, a bellows-mender; Thisby in the interlude
- Tom Snout, a tinker; Wall in the interlude
- Snug, a joiner; Lion in the interlude
- Robin Starveling, a tailor; Moonshine in the interlude

A WILLIAM
SHAKESPEARE'S
A
MIDSUMMER
NIGHT'S
DREAM

# VILLA ATHENA

*Day* — A grand Renaissance house nestled among a grove of vigilant cypress, atop a high hill in the Tuscan countryside. The main house is surrounded by farms and outbuildings. Vineyards and olive trees dress the terraced hillside below.

# FORMAL GARDEN

— Dominated by water and a huge statue of Neptune, servants work to line the formal garden with heavy walnut tables laid for a hundred guests—preparations for a noble wedding.

# KITCHEN

— A dozen cooks and scullery persons labor at the feast. Whole roast pigs, pollo, tacchino, bistecca Fiorentina. Mountains of garlic and onion, baskets of rosemary, basil, and thyme. Grilled peppers, yellow and red, swimming in olive oil and anchovies, braised fennel, grilled eggplant, delicate zucchini flowers and porcini mushrooms, like fairy umbrellas, grilled whole. Pastries made of chestnut, apricot, apple, and cream. And huge vats of pasta—fresh, dry—a sauce of tomato and pancetta, another of pesto. Table after table of the most lovable food in the world being prepared with an easy concentration by people to whom this is second nature.

# THEATER

— A little jewel of a place. Craftsmen are rebuilding the ducal box. Painters decorate the proscenium, the backdrop. A heavy wine red curtain is hoisted above the stage tied off at the corner with *putti* rampant and crowned in the center with a grinning mask of Bacchus.

# FORMAL GARDEN

*Day* — The preparations continue. The garden statuary is garlanded with laurel. Rows of banners line the cypress groves. Huge lilies are placed like boats inside the tiered fountains.

# BALCONY

— Surveying all this is DUKE THESEUS, winemaker, poet, hunter, warrior, statesman, lover, lord of all we've observed. He plucks a single white rose and exits the shot.

# BALCONY

— The beautiful HIPPOLYTA strolls dreamily among the summer vines and flowers, as preparations continue around her. THESEUS approaches from behind, rose in hand, and wraps his strong arms around her waist.

*Theseus offers Hippolyta a rose.*

**Theseus**  Now, fair Hippolyta, our nuptial hour
Draws on apace. Four happy days bring in
Another moon; but, O, methinks, how slow
This old moon wanes!

⟳ He has come nearer, nearer, his face almost touching hers.

**Theseus**  She lingers my desires,
Like to a stepdame, or a dowager,
Long withering out a young man's revenue.

⟳ And they kiss lightly, sweetly. She pulls away a little, but only to flirt.

**Hippolyta**  Four days will quickly steep themselves in night,
Four nights will quickly dream away the time;
And then the moon, like to a silver bow
New-bent in heaven, shall behold the night
Of our solemnities.

⟳ As their lips touch again, the sound of approaching footsteps.

**Egeus**  Happy be Theseus, our renowned Duke!

⟶ A lovely kiss, interrupted. THESEUS turns a little irritable toward a graying, bearded nobleman, EGEUS.

*Theseus*  Thanks, good Egeus. What's the news with thee?

⟶ We see now the older man's rage. He takes THESEUS aside.

*Egeus* (*v.o.*)  Full of vexation come I, with complaint
Against my child, my daughter Hermia.

# THESEUS' STUDY

⟶ Close on the worried face of HERMIA.

*Egeus*  Stand forth, Demetrius.

⟶ A handsome boy of twenty-two, clean-shaven, neatly trimmed, a little obsequious but largely unobjectionable.

*Egeus*  My noble lord,
This man hath my consent to marry her.
Stand forth, Lysander.

⟶ A second youth emerges, producing an audible gasp from HERMIA. His hair is long, his aspect poetical and a little fierce. THESEUS moves behind his writing desk. As he does, the young men take up positions on either side of EGEUS, giving the impromptu proceeding the appearance of a hearing or trial. EGEUS points an accusatory finger at LYSANDER.

*Egeus*  This man hath bewitched the bosom of my child.
Thou, thou, Lysander, thou hast given her rhymes

And interchanged love tokens with my child.
With cunning hast thou filched my daughter's heart,
Turned her obedience, which is *due to me,*
To stubborn harshness. And, my gracious Duke,
Be it so she will not here before your Grace
Consent to marry with Demetrius,
I beg the ancient privilege of Athens:

⟶ EGEUS places two large books, law books, on the desk before THESEUS. He opens each to a marked place.

*Egeus*  As she is mine, I may dispose of her,
Which shall be either to this gentleman
Or to her death, according to our law
Immediately provided in that case.

⟶ THESEUS glances at the book—not his favorite part of the job.

*Theseus*  What say you, Hermia?

⟶ There is a pause. Then HERMIA reaches out and takes LYSANDER's hand. DEMETRIUS can't bear it.

*Demetrius*  Relent, sweet Hermia: and Lysander, yield
Thy crazed title to my certain right.

*Lysander*  You have her father's love, Demetrius;
Let me have Hermia's: do you marry him.

⟶ This is too much. DEMETRIUS rushes LYSANDER, who sidesteps him and throws him into a table. He's up in a moment and they grapple awkwardly until attendants subdue them.

Demetrius and Lysander wait to hear Theseus' decision regarding Hermia's fate.

**Egeus** Scornful Lysander! True, he hath my love,
And what is mine my love shall render him.
And she is mine, and all my right of her
I do estate unto Demetrius.

⟿ LYSANDER pulls free of the attendants, throws himself toward THESEUS.

**Lysander** I am, my lord, as well derived as he,
As well possessed;

⟿ The attendants are on him in a moment but the plea in his eyes causes THESEUS to signal them away.

**Lysander** My love is more than his;
And, which is more than all these boasts can be,
I am beloved of beauteous Hermia.
Why should not I then prosecute my right?

⟿ THESEUS' attention is drawn suddenly to an open doorway. There stands Hippolyta watching him.

**Lysander** Demetrius, I'll avouch it to his head,
Made love to Nedar's daughter, Helena,
And won her soul; and she, sweet lady, dotes,
Devoutly dotes, dotes in idolatry,
Upon this spotted and inconstant man.

**Theseus** I must confess that I have heard so much . . .

⟿ A pause. THESEUS glances at HIPPOLYTA, realizes that nothing short of the wisdom of Solomon will impress his reluctant bride. He pauses, signals HERMIA to follow him.

# INNER CHAMBER

⟿ They sit across from each other in two Savanarola chairs.

**Theseus** Demetrius is a worthy gentleman.

**Hermia** So is Lysander.

**Theseus** In himself he is;
But in this case, wanting your father's voice,
The other must be held the worthier.

**Hermia** I would my father looked but with my eyes.

⟿ THESEUS pours her a glass of water.

**Theseus** Rather your eyes must with his judgment look.

**Hermia** I do entreat Your Grace to pardon me.
I know not by what power I am made bold,
Nor how it may concern my modesty
In such a presence here to plead my thoughts;
But I beseech Your Grace that I may know
The worst that may befall me in this case.

⟿ He hands her the law book open to the page. She reads a little, blanches.

**Theseus** Either to die the death, or to abjure
Forever the society of men.
Therefore, fair Hermia, question your desires;
Know of your youth, examine well your blood,
Whether, if you yield not to your father's choice,
You can endure the livery of a nun,

For aye to be in shady cloister mewed,
To live a barren sister all your life,
Chanting faint hymns to the cold fruitless moon.

⌁ Close on HERMIA.

*Hermia*  So will I grow, so live, so die,
　my lord,
Ere I will yield my virgin patent up
Unto his lordship, whose unwished yoke
My soul consents not to give sovereignty.

*Theseus*  Take time to pause—

⌁ But HERMIA shakes her head. She will
take no time. She needs no time.

# STUDY

⌁ THESEUS stands behind his desk, makes
his pronouncement. She has given him no
choice.

*Theseus* (cont.)  . . . by the next new moon
Upon that day either prepare to die
For disobedience to your father's will
Or else to wed Demetrius as he would,
Or on Diana's altar to protest
For aye austerity and single life.

⌁ He slams the book shut, practically
throws it at EGEUS, who alone is perverse
enough to find this pleasing. He looks at
HIPPOLYTA. He walks to the door.

*Theseus* (cont.) Demetrius, come;
And come, Egeus. You shall go with me.

⌁ HERMIA and LYSANDER sit, stunned,
together.

*Theseus* (cont.)  For you, fair Hermia, look
　you arm yourself
To fit your fancies to your father's will;
Come, my Hippolyta. What cheer, my love?

⌁ But she turns and walks away. THESEUS
is making no headway there at all.

*Theseus* (defeated)  Demetrius and Egeus,
　go along.
I have some private schooling for you both.

⌁ DEMETRIUS and EGEUS have no choice
but to follow THESEUS, leaving the lovers
alone. LYSANDER reaches toward his HERMIA,
gently strokes her hair.

*Lysander*  How now, my love! Why is
　your cheek so pale?
How chance the roses there do fade so fast?

*Hermia*  Belike for want of rain, which I
　could well
Beteem them from the tempest of my eyes.

⌁ LYSANDER leads her toward the frescoed
walls.

*Lysander*  Ay me! For aught that I could
　ever read,
Could ever hear by tale or history,
The course of true love never did run smooth.

⌁ The next shot is over the fresco's images
from the *Metamorphoses*. Apollo's fruitless pursuit
of Daphne. The death of Procris at her lover's
unwitting hand. Thisby's unfortunate suicide.

*Lysander* (v.o.)  If there were a sympathy
　in choice,
War, death, or sickness did lay siege to it,
Making it momentary as a sound,

Swift as a shadow, short as any dream
And ere a man hath power to say "Behold!"
The jaws of darkness do devour it up:

⟿ He holds her close.

*Lysander*  So quick bright things come to
   confusion.
Therefore, hear me Hermia . . .

⟿ He lowers his voice. A plan . . .

# CORRIDOR

⟿ DEMETRIUS stands a little apart watching
THESEUS and EGEUS engage in a heated
argument. We can't make out what they say
but will assume THESEUS is trying to convince
the old man to relent. Then another voice
floats in at the window.

*Voice* (o.s.)  Demetrius. Demetrius.

⟿ DEMETRIUS crosses to the open window.
There below stands a damp and bedraggled
young woman who brightens visibly when
she sees him.

*Helena*  Demetrius.

⟿ DEMETRIUS looks nervously in the direction of his elders and motions her away.
Closing the window, he disappears from view.

# FORMAL GARDEN

*Day* ⟿ HELENA kicks at the muddy
ground in frustration. Picks up her bike,
which leans against the wall.

*Helena*  How happy some o'er other
   some can be!
Through Athens I am thought as fair as she.
But what of that? Demetrius thinks *not* so;
He will not know what all but he do know.
Love looks not with the eyes, but with the
   mind,
And therefore is winged Cupid painted blind.

⟿ As she passes a covered staircase,
HERMIA and LYSANDER emerge.

*Hermia*  God speed fair Helena! Whither
   away?

⟿ HELENA looks at her for a long
disbelieving moment.

*Helena*  Call you me fair? That fair again
   unsay.
Demetrius loves your fair. O happy fair!
Sickness is catching. O, were favor so,
Yours would I catch, fair Hermia, ere I go;
O, teach me how you look, and with what art
You sway the motion of Demetrius' heart!

*Hermia*  His folly Helena is no fault of
   mine.

*Helena*  None but your beauty: would
   that fault were mine!

*Hermia*  Take comfort. He no more shall
   see my face.

⟿ HELENA is puzzled. HERMIA and
LYSANDER exchange a conspiratorial smile and
lead her into a nearby grotto.

(Note that the grotto is decorated with
statues of three Bacchic figures: a man
and a woman, beautiful, exquisite bodies,

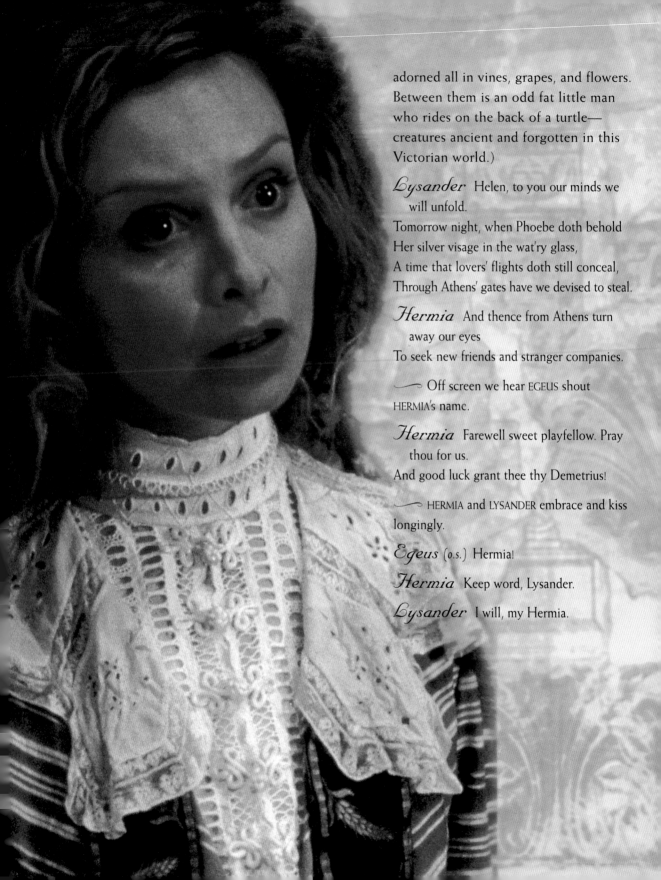

adorned all in vines, grapes, and flowers.
Between them is an odd fat little man
who rides on the back of a turtle—
creatures ancient and forgotten in this
Victorian world.)

*Lysander*  Helen, to you our minds we
    will unfold.
Tomorrow night, when Phoebe doth behold
Her silver visage in the wat'ry glass,
A time that lovers' flights doth still conceal,
Through Athens' gates have we devised to steal.

*Hermia*  And thence from Athens turn
    away our eyes
To seek new friends and stranger companies.

⟶ Off screen we hear EGEUS shout
HERMIA's name.

*Hermia*  Farewell sweet playfellow. Pray
    thou for us.
And good luck grant thee thy Demetrius!

⟶ HERMIA and LYSANDER embrace and kiss
longingly.

*Egeus*  (o.s.) Hermia!

*Hermia*  Keep word, Lysander.

*Lysander*  I will, my Hermia.

They kiss once again. HELENA has to watch, again. HERMIA with tears in her eyes backs away from LYSANDER slowly, then turns and runs. LYSANDER, equally caught up in the emotion, forgets for a moment that HELENA even exists. She clears her throat. LYSANDER comes to.

*Lysander*  Helena, adieu.
As you on him, Demetrius dote on you!

He disappears into the garden. HELENA watches him for a long moment then plops down next to the little Bacchus.

*Helena*  O, spite!

She begins to weep. A fountain in the floor comes on, drenching her.

*Helena*  O, hell!

The statues seem almost to study her misery. Cut to:

# CHURCH TOWER

*Evening*  The bells of the cathedral and all her seven sister churches ring out, celebrating the end of mass in the little village of Monte Athena.

# MONTE ATHENA

The walled village perched on the crown of a high Tuscan hill.

# STREET

A series of posters being slapped up on a stone wall, announcing, one after another, a theatrical competition for the right to perform at the wedding of His Grace, DUKE THESEUS. Those chosen, it points out, if they perform well, will be rewarded with a small pension.

# PIAZZA

The central square is filling now with the citizenry. It is the hour of the promenade, the opportunity to talk, to flirt, to cut *la bella figura*. A large crowd, LYSANDER among them, gathers around a traveling vendor, a seller of bicycles, huge advertisements, nothing but bicycles. He hands the proprietor a sizable chunk of change and wheels away not one, but two.

PETER QUINCE, a small bespectacled gentleman, greets and is greeted as he makes his way across the piazza. He carries a pile of play scripts in his hands.

Near the center of the square, he notices a troupe of acting students being led in rehearsal by a thin-faced, ungenerous schoolteacher. This is MASTER ANTONIO.

# ADJACENT STREET

The open market is breaking up. TOM SNOUT the tinker closes up his vending cart, drags it tinkling and jingling away.

*Helena, determined to win Demetrius' love.*

UMBRELLAS AND
FADED AWNINGS

MARKET ~ PIAZZA

# CITY STREET

⟳ SNUG the joiner, short, soft-spoken, maker of wooden toys and figurines, and the tailor, old ROBIN STARVELING, emerge from their two small workshops across the road from each other. A scroungy little terrier yaps at STARVELING's feet as they head up the inclined cobbles to the square and the evening's adventure.

# ANTICO CAFFE GRECO

⟳ The finest in the piazza: the young men treat their girls to ice cream, the old men guzzle Chianti and play *briscola*. Admiring himself in the window, drinking Campari in an immaculate

white suit, is NICK BOTTOM. Finishing his drink, he picks up his hat and walking stick and starts across the Piazza.

Into the fresh, cool evening. Two very beautiful girls pass. BOTTOM tips his hat to them and they smile. Then he catches something out of the corner of his eye. A woman, shrewish, her beady eyes search the square. He ducks inside the bar hoping to avoid detection.

# PIAZZA

⟳ Outside the cathedral, on its grand steps, have assembled the carpenter, PETER QUINCE, precise and organized, young FRANCIS FLUTE the bellows mender, SNUG, and STARVELING.

**Quince** Is all our company here?

— TOM SNOUT lugs his cart along, out of breath with the effort. He parks it next to a donkey tethered to a stone stanchion.

**Snout** Here, Peter Quince.

— While from the other side of the square comes BOTTOM. As he waves to his fellows, he passes MASTER ANTONIO, who stands with a couple of dangerous-looking twelve-year-olds. He points after BOTTOM, whispers something to them and hands each a one hundred lire coin.

BOTTOM joins his group of friends. They exchange greetings. QUINCE calls for attention.

**Quince** Here is—

**Bottom** First, good Peter Quince, say what the play treats on; then read the names of the actors; and so grow to a point.

**Quince** Marry, our play is, "The most lamentable comedy, and most cruel death of Pyramus and Thisby."

— STARVELING's little terrier yaps in approval.

**Bottom** A very good piece of work, I assure you,

*The hour of the Promenade in the Piazza.*

*Bottom rehearses his lines.*

and a merry. Now, good Peter Quince, call forth your actors by the scroll.

⟶ BOTTOM is very conscious of the crowd that is gathering, especially the two beauties he saw earlier who now, having made their evening's *passegiata*, are arrived just here.

*Quince*  Here is—

⟶ BOTTOM gestures flamboyantly at the paper QUINCE holds in his hand.

*Bottom*  . . . the scroll of every man's name, which is thought fit, through all Athens, to play in
our interlude before the Duke and the Duchess, on his wedding day at night.

⟶ And needing just a little more space to present himself . . .

*Bottom*  Masters, spread yourselves.

⟶ The dangerous twelve-year-olds come closer. QUINCE refers to his scroll.

*Quince*  Answer as I call you, Nick Bottom the weaver.

⟶ BOTTOM swaggers up a couple of steps, smiles at the ladies.

*Bottom*  Ready. Name what part I am for, and proceed.

*Quince*  You, Nick Bottom, are set down for Pyramus.

*Bottom*  What is Pyramus? A lover, or a tyrant?

*Quince*  A lover that kills himself, most gallant, for love.

⟶ BOTTOM gives this very serious consideration.

*Bottom*  That will ask some tears in the true performing
of it: if I do it, let the audience look to their eyes. Yet my chief humor is for a tyrant. I could play Ercles rarely,

> *"The raging rocks*
> *And shivering shocks*
> *Shall break the locks*
> *Of prison gates;"*

⟶ STARVELING's little dog nips at his pant leg. He pushes it away with his foot.

*Bottom*  *"And Phibbus' car*
> *Shall shine from far,*
> *And make and mar*
> *The foolish Fates."*

⟶ He takes a bow to a smattering of applause and at least one very pleasant smile. To QUINCE:

*Bottom*  That was lofty!

⟶ Feigning exhaustion, he moves down to a nearby fountain. He drinks and on his way back passes near to the girls.

*Bottom*  (*whispers*)  This is Ercles' vein, a tyrant's vein. A lover is
more condoling.

⟶ QUINCE shakes his head, tries to keep it together.

*Quince*  Francis Flute, the bellows mender.

*Flute*  Here, Peter Quince.

*"Bottom is a weaver by trade, but he is an artist at heart. The urge to ally himself to ideas or representations of an heroic or transcendent nature is one of the defining principles of his character. I think there is a little of Bottom in every actor."*
*—Kevin Kline*

The mechanicals discuss their parts in the play they are preparing for the wedding night of the Duke and the Duchess: (left to right) Quince, Flute, Snout, Starveling.

Bottom at the hour of the promenade in the Piazza is excited to learn what role he has been chosen to play.

⟶ But he says it in such a sweet and quiet voice that QUINCE doesn't hear him.

**Quince** Francis Flute, the bellows mender!

⟶ Having missed the fact that FLUTE is right next to him, QUINCE continues to try to locate him. Meanwhile, the two twelve-year-olds pilfer a canvas bag from SNOUT's cart and begin scooping errant donkey droppings into it. Having found him . . .

**Quince** Francis Flute, you must take Thisby on you.

**Flute** What is Thisby? A wand'ring knight?

**Quince** It is the lady that Pyramus must love.

⟶ A laugh from the crowd.

**Flute** Nay, faith, let not me play a woman. I have
a beard coming.

**Bottom** An I may hide my face, let me play Thisby too,
I'll speak in a monstrous little voice "Thisne, Thisne!" "Ah Pyramus, my lover dear! Thy Thisby dear, and lady dear!"

⟶ He has the crowd in stitches.

**Quince** No, no; you must play Pyramus: and, Flute,
you Thisby. Robin Starveling, the tailor.

**Starveling** Here, Peter Quince.

⟶ QUINCE hands out the parts of the lovers' fathers. Meanwhile we pan the boys, with their dung bag, by a small door at the base of the belltower.

**Quince** Snug, the joiner; you, the lion's part. And
I hope here we have a play fitted.

**Snug** Have you the lion's part written? Pray you, if
it be, give it me, for I am slow of study.

**Bottom** Let me play the lion too. I will roar that I
will do any man's heart good to hear me.

⌐ He roars and the crowd responds enthusiastically.

**Bottom** I will roar, that I will make the

Duke say, "Let him roar again, let him roar again."

⌐ The crowd shouts for more.

**Quince** An you should do it too terribly, you would
fright the Duchess and the ladies, that they would
shriek; and that were enough to hang us all.

⌐ Worried looks course 'round BOTTOM'S fellow actors.

**Snout** That would hang us, every mother's son.

**Bottom** I grant you, friends, if I should fright the ladies out of their wits,

they would have no more discretion but to
     hang us: but I will aggravate
my voice so that I will roar you as gently as any
sucking dove.

⟋ To the delight of the audience, he
demonstrates. He doesn't realize the boys are
poised above him at the top of the tower,
their bag at the ready; they begin to tip the
contents out as . . .

*Bottom*  I will roar you an 'twere any
     nightingale.

⟋ And it's a direct hit. BOTTOM finds
himself, his hair, his white suit, even his
waxed moustache covered in donkey manure.
The audience turns on him on a dime—they
turn, laughing uproariously at his misfortune.
Atop the portico, the two boys bray like a
     couple of asses gone mad. BOTTOM
     moves back under the portico, humil-
     iated. QUINCE approaches him,
     begins to brush him off, speaks to
     him gently and tries to comfort
     him.

     *Quince*  You can play
     no part but Pyramus.

     ⟋ The crowd senses
     the show is over and
     begins to disband.

     *Quince*  Pyramus is
     a sweet-faced man; a
     proper man as

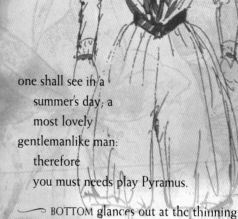

one shall see in a
     summer's day; a
     most lovely
gentlemanlike man:
     therefore
     you must needs play Pyramus.

⟋ BOTTOM glances out at the thinning
crowd. The pretty girl looks back once (was
it pity?) before disappearing into the dusky
twilight.

*Bottom*  Well, I will undertake it.

⟋ QUINCE nods, "Good, very good," turns
to the others.

*Quince*  Masters, here are your parts; and I
     am to entreat you
to con them by tomorrow night and meet in
     the palace wood,
a mile without the town. There will we rehearse.

⟋ They look at him quizzically. QUINCE
indicates MASTER ANTONIO, who watches
them, a smug smile on his face.

*Quince*  If we meet in the city, we shall be
     dogged with company
and our devices known.

*QUINCE singles out* BOTTOM.

*Quince* I pray you fail me not.

*Bottom* (*takes his hand*) We will meet; and
there we may rehearse
most obscenely and courageously.

*BOTTOM picks up his walking stick,
replaces his hat, doing his best to pop up his battered dignity. He walks away across the square.*

*Bottom* Take pains; be perfect; adieu.

*The others watch him go,* QUINCE *a
little more sadly than the rest.*

# STAIRCASE

*Night* *BOTTOM lets himself into a
squalid ground floor entry and makes his way
slowly up the dark stairs.*

# BOTTOM'S FLAT

*Night* *BOTTOM enters as quietly as
possible into a squalid little room. His* WIFE,
*the shrew from the square, appears. She looks
at him with contempt, makes a noise,
something between a grunt and a growl.
Almost immediately a baby begins to cry.*

BOTTOM *slowly takes off his suit, placing it in a
makeshift closet. The closet is almost empty.
It is clearly the only suit he owns. (One
remembers now that Italy is the only country
in the world where a man is willing to go into*

debt to buy clothes.) He puts the hat and walking stick carefully away and lies down on the bed. He stares at a spot of damp on the ceiling. The baby continues to cry.

Cut to:

# CITY STREET

*Day* — Rain. People rush to their destinations, black umbrellas dot the wet cobbles.

# WEAVING SHOP

*Day* — BOTTOM sits at his loom, staring out at the rain. From his POV, a young woman, dripping wet, passes by the window.

# CITY STREET

*Day* — It is HELENA, too deeply distracted by thoughts of DEMETRIUS to mind the rain.

*Helena* . . . ere Demetrius looked on Hermia's eyne,
He hailed down oaths that he was only mine;

— She has to excuse herself for running into an old woman who drops her shopping. HELENA is too obsessed even to help.

*Helena* And when this hail some heat from Hermia felt,
So he dissolved and showers of oath did melt.

— Suddenly, it strikes her.

*Helena* I will go tell him of fair Hermia's flight.

— Cut to:

# CITY GATES

*Late evening* — DEMETRIUS bicycles through the Porta Romana (there's always a Porta Romana). As he does, another rider emerges from the shadowy stone wall. HELENA's voice continues over as we recognize her bedraggled form.

*Helena* (*v.o.*) For herein mean I to enrich my pain.
To have his sight thither and back again.

— She pedals fiercely down the road after him, her dark cloak trailing behind. Lightning flashes overhead as we . . .

Cut to:

# DEEP FOREST

*Night* — The flash reveals a huge stone mask, its monstrous mouth agape— large enough to walk through, to ride a bike through. A portal? A gateway?

*Helena* (*v.o.*) Then to the wood will he this very night pursue her.

— And now deeper in the forest. Lightning among the trees reflects in the puddles and pools left behind by the rain. Little incandescent creatures (fireflies) flit among the dark trees. Another flash reveals the outline of an odd little creature as it disappears into a hold, a cave in an adjacent cliff face. Following it into the darkness we find ourselves . . .

Cut to:

# FAIRY BAR

*Night* — Once an Etruscan tomb painted around with delicate figures of athletes, runners, and divers, it now mirrors in its function the caffè in the square. The clientele however . . . we pull back to reveal . . . a table of bearded sinewy dwarves playing at an ancient chesslike game. In little boothlike indentations, elegant fairies and satyrs carouse together. A frightening goat-headed creature, red-eyed and angry, bellows for service. In one corner a small, winged dwarflike thing repairs the injured wing of his fellow. A fat little satyr approaches a pond filled with water nymphs, whispery, giggling, naked as the day of their generation. A fire burns, food is served and prepared by old women draped in black. A group of three old fawns pounds metal into cups and bowls.

At a small table sits a short chubby creature, hair pulled up in a topknot, head ringed in vines. He downs a glass of a brown beery substance and pours another. This is PUCK. He looks up as a tired-eyed female fairy, COBWEB, makes her exhausted way across the bar.

*Puck* How now, spirit! Whither wander you?

— He offers the little creature to sit. She virtually collapses into the chair, thoroughly disaffected.

*Cobweb* Over hill, over dale,
Thorough bush, thorough brier,
Over park, over pale,
Thorough flood, thorough fire,
I do wander *everywhere*,
Swifter than the moon's sphere,
And I serve the Fairy Queen,
To dew her orbs upon the green.

— PUCK offers her a drink. She shakes her head, gestures to some shady characters at a nearby table.

*Cobweb* I must go seek some dewdrops here,
And hang a pearl in every cowslip's ear.

— She starts to go but looks back at PUCK, "Wait a minute."

*Cobweb* Either I mistake your shape and making quite,
Or else you are that shrewd and knavish sprite
Called Robin Goodfellow.

— He shrugs, but it's obviously false modesty. COBWEB takes the drink after all.

*Cobweb* Are not you he
That frights the maidens of the villagery,
Skim milk, and sometimes labor in the quern,
And bootless make the breathless housewife churn.

— She signals others to the table.

*Cobweb*  Are you not he?

— PUCK pauses for effect.

*Puck*  Thou speakest aright;
I am that merry wanderer of the night.

— This to a chorus of approval and several handshakes.

*Puck*  I jest to Oberon and make him smile,
When I a fat and bean-fed horse beguile,
Neighing in likeness of a filly foal:

— We push in on PUCK's face.

*Puck*  . . . And sometimes lurk I in a
     gossip's bowl
In very likeness of a roasted crab,
And when she drinks, against her lips I bob,
And on her withered dewlap pour the ale.

— The fairies laugh. All save one who lets

out a squeal. We cut in to reveal a tiny PUCK swimming in her drink. The creature throws the glass to the floor.

Whip pan to: PUCK back at his chair.

*Puck* (cont.)  And sometimes . . .

# FATTORIA

— A huge FOREMAN wears on his close-cropped bristly head an orange and yellow skullcap, drives a smaller worker from the stone barn with blow after blow. He shouts at him in Italian, "You no good lazy pig."

Cutting out we see PUCK sitting on the edge of a well, watching. He blows a handful of dust in the direction of the man.

The fairy bar.

The peasant covers his head to protect himself. The blows quit coming. He looks at the place where the FOREMAN stood and sees staring back at him a boar, a wild pig—wearing an orange and yellow skullcap.

A couple of farmhands come running, hunting rifles at the ready. The enchanted FOREMAN runs for the woods hoping to escape with his piggy life. PUCK sits in an olive tree laughing and laughing.

## FAIRY BAR

*Night* — And the fairies laugh with him.

## CROSSROADS

*Night* — More thunder, more lightning. PUCK and COBWEB exit the bar, arms around each other's very drunken shoulders. PUCK pulls away to pee against a tree.

*Cobweb* Farewell, thou lob of spirits; I'll be gone.
Our Queen and all her elves come here anon.

— She points to the cliff face, where we see a train of figures veiled in white. They carry at their center a litter draped in silk, glowing with warm light from within.

"The choice of Italy led me to the Etruscans. Their interest in beauty, music, magic, divination, sensuality, their unapologetic vanity, and their reverence for the feminine made them excellent models for the fairy world. This was especially true in contrast to the uptight, conventional world of the court. Luciana Arrighi, the production designer, and I visited all the great Etruscan museums. We based props on interesting bronze objects we saw. We studied tomb painting and drew on the burnt sienna and olive greens of the frescoed walls. Props, costumes, and sets all took Etruria as their starting point."
—Michael Hoffman, Director

*Puck* (over his shoulder) The King doth keep
his revels here tonight.
Take heed the Queen come not within his sight.
For Oberon is passing fell and wrath.

⟿ Then it happens. The wind comes up.
The ground begins to rumble. The water boils
in the pond. PUCK and COBWEB look at each
other. The little firefly creatures scatter and hide.

# FAIRY BAR

*Night* ⟿ The nymphs stop laughing.
The satyrs stop flirting. The dwarves stop
drinking, pick up their tools, and leave.

# CROSSROADS

*Night* ⟿ The deep rumbling grows,
but the procession of veiled women carries on
undaunted. A frightened PUCK dives under a
rocky shelf. Louder the rumbling gets as the
women approach the heart of OBERON's
domain. Lightning strikes the path and the
women stop. At its source, glorious OBERON
the Fairy King, seated above them in a throne
cut out of a rocky cliff, his head wound
around with grapevines and laurel leaves.
Sphynxes crouch on either side of him.

*Oberon* Ill met by moonlight, proud Titania.

*Titania* What, jealous Oberon! Fairy, skip
hence.
I have forsworn his bed and company.

*Oberon* Tarry rash wanton. Am I not thy
lord?

*Titania* Then I must be thy lady.

⟿ The curtain is drawn back to reveal the
exquisite beauty of the FAIRY QUEEN.

*Titania* Why art thou here,
Come from the farthest steep of India?
But that, forsooth, the bouncing Amazon,
Your buskined mistress and your warrior love,
To Theseus must be wedded, and you come
To give their bed joy and prosperity.

*Oberon* How canst thou thus for shame,
Titania,
Glance at my credit with Hippolyta,
Knowing I know thy love to Theseus?

*Titania* These are the forgeries of jealousy:
And never, since the middle summer's spring,
Met we on hill, in dale, forest, or mead,
By paved fountain or by rushy brook,
But with thy brawls thou has disturbed our sport.
Therefore the winds, piping to us in vain,
As in revenge, have sucked up from the sea.

# VINEYARDS, FIELDS, PASTURES

⟿ Everywhere there is rain, an apocalyptic
downpour. Water falls on water, and beneath
the surface, the ruined remains of domestic life.

*Titania* (v.o.) Contagious fogs, which,
falling in the land,
Hath every pelting river made so proud,
That they have overborne their continent.

⟿ The rain pelts the vines, driving the
grapes to the ground, knocking the young
olives from the olive trees.

Puck at the fairy bar.

**Titania** *(v.o.)* The fold stands empty in the drowned field,
And crows are fatted with the murrion flock.

## A FLOODED ROAD

**Night** — And beneath the murky water of the pool, the decaying body of a sheep that never found its way home.

**Titania** *(v.o.)* And thorough this distemperature we see
The seasons alter: the spring, the summer,
The childing autumn, angry winter, change
Their wonted liveries; and the mazed world,
By their increase, now knows not which is which.

## CROSSROADS

**Night** — TITANIA, puffed up and fully the Queen, builds to her crescendo.

**Titania** And this same progeny of evils comes
From our debate, from our dissension;
We are their parents and original.

**Oberon** Do you amend it, then; it lies in you.

— OBERON is suddenly beside her.
A chorus of clicking and hissing goes up from her entourage. OBERON is unfazed.

*Oberon presides court over his fairies.*

**Oberon**  Why should Titania cross her
   Oberon?
I do but beg a little changeling boy,
To be my henchman.

**Titania**  Set your heart at rest.
The fairy land buys not the child of me.

⟶ She signals, and the child is led forward
on his pony. Adorned in gold, his skin is the
deep blue of the young god Krishna. Both
child and animal are canopied with flowers.
He comes near her and smiles as she gently
strokes his hair.

**Titania** (cont.)  His mother was a vot'ress
   of my order,
And, in the spiced Indian air, by night,
Full often hath she gossiped by my side,
And sat with me on Neptune's yellow sands.

⟶ She studies the little boy's beautiful
face, seeing her dear friend's visage. Her eyes
fill with tears.

**Titania** (cont.)  Marking th' embarked
   traders on the flood;
When we have laughed to see the sails conceive
And grow big-bellied with the wanton wind.

❧ 25 ❧

Titania
and the Changeling
Boy, who is the
source of Titania's
feud with Oberon.

She kisses the boy, strokes his raven hair, and signals for his escort to take him. She lowers her voice.

*Titania* (cont.) But she, being mortal, of that boy did die;
And for her sake do I rear up her boy,
And for her sake I will not part with him.

*Oberon* How long within this wood intend you stay?

*Titania* (softening a little) Perchance till after Theseus' wedding day.
If you will patiently dance in our round,
And see our moonlight revels, go with us.

*Oberon* Give me that boy, and I will go with thee.

TITANIA hisses at him. OBERON recoils. He looks up to find TITANIA and her fairies high up on the cliff's face.

*Titania* (outraged) Not for thy fairy kingdom. Fairies, away!
We shall chide downright, if I longer stay.

She and all her entourage disappear.

*Oberon* Well, go thy way. Thou shalt not from this grove
Till I torment thee for this injury.
My gentle Puck, come hither.

A pause, then a sheepish PUCK emerges from his foxhole. "The greater part of valor is discretion." OBERON takes him under his arm.

"The image of Titania is directly influenced by the works of Burne-Jones, G. F. Watts, and the Pre-Raphaelites."
—Michael Hoffman, Director

**Oberon** Thou rememb'rest
Since once I sat upon a promontory,
And heard a mermaid, on a dolphin's back,
Uttering such dulcet and harmonious breath,
That the rude sea grew civil at her song.

**Puck** I remember.

**Oberon** That very time I saw, but thou
    couldst not,
Flying between the cold moon and the earth,
Cupid all armed.

## CHAMBER

— A frescoed wall on which is depicted a
Cupid ready to let fly his love dart.

**Oberon** (v.o.) A certain aim he took
At a fair vestal throned by the west,
And loosed his love shaft smartly from his bow.

## FIELD

— Falling toward a field of white flowers.
An arrow strikes the ground.

**Oberon** (v.o.) Yet marked I where the bolt
    of Cupid fell.
It fell upon a little western flower,
Before milk-white, now purple with love's
    wound,
And maidens call it love-in-idleness.

— Close on a spring of red that bubbles up
among the flowers. As we pull back to reveal:
The white flowers have all gone deep red.

**Oberon** (v.o.) Fetch me that flow'r.

## CROSSROADS

**Night** — PUCK isn't quite following.

**Oberon** The juice of it on sleeping eyelids
    laid
Will make or man or woman madly dote
Upon the next live creature that it sees.
Fetch me this herb, and be thou here again
Ere the leviathan can swim a league.

**Puck** I'll put a girdle round about the earth
In forty minutes.

— PUCK takes a running jump into an
earthy bank. The surface of the ground is
suddenly alive, something tunneling very
rapidly. The tunnel travels in a circle around
OBERON then tears off across the wood at high
speed. We push in on OBERON.

**Oberon** Having once this juice,
I'll watch Titania when she is asleep,
And drop the liquor of it in her eyes.
The next thing then she waking looks upon,
She shall pursue it with the soul of love.
And ere I take this charm from off her sight,
I'll make her render up her page to me.

— His reverie is interrupted by a great noise
of crashing and whining. Is it TITANIA's return?

We pan away to find DEMETRIUS riding toward
us on his bicycle. By the time we pan back,
OBERON is gone. He hops off to check a low
tire. HELENA, not the greatest cyclist, bumps
over a rough patch and appears at his side.

**Demetrius** I love thee not, therefore pursue me not.
Where is Lysander and fair Hermia?

— He looks for tracks, scans the trees, then begins annoyedly to pump air into his tire.

**Demetrius** Thou told'st me they were stol'n unto this wood;
And here am I, and wood within this wood,
Because I cannot meet my Hermia.
Hence, get thee gone, and follow me no more!

— He looks over to find her mooning at him.

**Demetrius** Do I entice you? Do I speak you fair?
Or, rather, do I not in plainest truth
Tell you, I do not nor I cannot love you?

**Helena** And even for that do I love you the more.

— She squats awkwardly beside him.

**Helena** I am your spaniel; and, Demetrius,
The more you beat me, I will fawn on you.
Use me but as your spaniel, spurn me, strike me,
Neglect me, lose me; only give me leave,
Unworthy as I am, to follow you.
What worser place can I beg in your love—
Than to be used as you use your dog?

— OBERON can't help but wince. DEMETRIUS stands up and starts wheeling his bike away. HELENA follows.

**Demetrius** Tempt not too much the hatred of my spirit,

For I am sick when I do look on thee.

**Helena** And I am sick when I look not on you.

— DEMETRIUS stops, dismounts, and puts his kickstand down.

**Demetrius** You do impeach your modesty too much,
To leave the city, and commit yourself
Into the hands of one that loves you not.

— He seizes the handlebars of her bike and pushes her slowly backward. His tone becomes seductive. Surprised, she allows herself to roll back.

**Demetrius** To trust the opportunity of night
And the ill counsel of a desert place
With the rich worth of your virginity.

— HELENA puts her feet down, stopping the backward motion.

**Helena** Your virtue is my privilege: for that
It is not night when I do see your face,
Therefore I think I am not in the night.

— And now she becomes the aggressor. She backs DEMETRIUS up as though the two were engaged in a strange tango.

**Helena** Nor doth this wood lack worlds of company,
For you in my respect are all the world.

— His plan having blown up in his face, DEMETRIUS runs for his bicycle.

**Demetrius** I'll run from thee and hide me in the brakes,

And leave thee to the mercy of wild beasts.

*Helena*  The wildest hath not such a heart
as you.
Run when you will, the story shall be
changed:
Apollo flies, and Daphne holds the chase;
The dove pursues the griffin.

⌒ DEMETRIUS pedals ahead, flying over a
series of nasty bumps.

*Demetrius*  I will not stay thy questions.
Let me go!
Or, if thou follow me, do not believe
But I shall do thee mischief in the wood.

⌒ He comes over a rise and flies down a
hill and by camera.

*Helena*  Ay, in the temple, in the town,
the field,
You do me mischief.

⌒ DEMETRIUS somehow manages to
negotiate the puddle at the bottom. HELENA
doesn't and ends ass over teakettle in the
muck. She looks up, face covered in mud.

*Helena*  Fie, Demetrius!
Your wrongs do set a scandal on my sex.
We cannot fight for love, as men may do;
We should be woo'd, and were not made to
woo.

⌒ As she watches him disappear, she pulls
herself together as best she can.

*Helena*  I'll follow thee, and make a
heaven of hell,
To die upon the hand I love so well.

⌒ Close on OBERON, who watches her
ride clumsily away from his rocky perch.

*Oberon*  Fare thee well, nymph: ere he do
leave this grove,
Thou shalt fly him, and he shall seek thy love.

⌒ OBERON looks down to see PUCK's
moving molehill speeding toward him.

*Oberon*  Hast thou the flower there?

⌒ The flower pops up through the earth
as if it had grown there. OBERON is suddenly
on the ground beside it. He plucks the flower.

*Oberon*  I know a bank where the wild
thyme blows,

⌒ The camera cranes up and over the
throne as we dissolve to:

# FOREST

*Night* ⌒ The camera travels high
above a dense forest.

*Oberon* (v.o.)  Where oxlips and the
nodding violet grows,
Quite overcanopied with luscious woodbine,
With sweet roses, and with eglantine.

⌒ Dissolve to:

# TITANIA'S BOWER

*Night* ⌒ The camera climbs over the
flowery ridge to reveal the FAIRY QUEEN and
her entourage in amongst the walls of an
antique ruin, crowned by a broken stoned

dome, like something out of Piranesi. A series of arched windows line the back; trees grow up among the moss-encrusted walls.

**Oberon** (v.o.) There sleeps Titania sometime of the night,
Lulled in these flowers with dances and delight.

⌒ And across the little valley, crouched low against the opposite ridge, PUCK and OBERON spy on her. OBERON holds the red flower in his hand.

**Oberon** . . . with the juice of this I'll streak her eyes,
And make her full of hateful fantasies.

⌒ He plucks a couple of scarlet petals and hands them to PUCK.

**Oberon** Take thou some of it.

⌒ PUCK holds up his hand, asking the KING to pause. He takes out a notebook and a quill pen. "Ready."

**Oberon** . . . and seek through this grove.
A sweet Athenian lady is in love
With a disdainful youth. Anoint his eyes;
But do it when the next thing he espies
May be the lady. Thou shalt know the man
By the Athenian garments he has on.

⌒ PUCK nods. He's got it.

**Oberon** And look thou meet me ere the first cock crow.

⌒ As he hurries away down the hill . . .

**Puck** Fear not, my lord, your servant shall do so.

⌒ OBERON turns his attention to this wife of his. Her world is a gentle one; colorful, androgynous creatures gather 'round a crystal clear pond to marvel at their reflections. They admire each other's beauty and laugh. A young fairy, MOTH, repairs the diaphanous wing of her companion, MUSTARDSEED. In one corner, two nymphs consult the milky-eyed, Medusalike priestess. In another, three young women, THE FATES, perform their never-ending tasks—spinning, measuring, and cutting the thread of life.

Seeing all is well, TITANIA climbs into her bed, a large sunken affair, a little like a small barge. It is hung with ivy and filled with flowers.

**Titania** Sing me now asleep.
Then to your offices, and let me rest.

⌒ A band of her veiled handmaidens begin to play on exotic instruments our exotic props person invented.

Four of TITANIA's entourage fix cranks into the stone wall from which the bed is suspended. They turn them. A hoist is set in motion, the action of which is raising her bed slowly into a protective canopy of trees.

The music soothes and soon TITANIA is asleep. A signal is given from PEASEBLOSSOM, perched in the arched opening above, to a fairy guard, COBWEB, on the ground.

**Cobweb** Hence, away! Now all is well.
One aloof stand sentinel.

⌒ And above her shines the vigilant moon.

Oberon explains to Puck how to cast the spell.

## FOREST

*Night* — MECHANICALS make their way toward their secret rehearsal. Torches light their way.

*Bottom*  What beard were I best to play it in?

*Quince*  What you will.

*Bottom*  I will discharge it in either your straw-color beard,
Your orange-tawny beard, your purple-in-grain beard . . .

— They walk through the stone gate, the creature's mouth, passing unconsciously through the portal, into the fairy world.

## TITANIA'S BOWER

*Night* — Cutting to TITANIA's sentinel on the ruined wall. OBERON appears at her side. She's about to sound the alarm when he holds up a bronze mirror, richly decorated. Enchanted by her own image, almost hypnotized, she takes the mirror, forgetting all else.

OBERON crouches over the sleeping QUEEN and squeezes the love juice onto her eyelids.

*Oberon*  What thou seest when thou dost wake,
Do it for thy truelove take;
Love and languish for his sake.
Be it ounce, or cat, or bear,
Pard, or boar with bristled hair,
In thy eye that shall appear

When thou wak'st, it is thy dear.

⟶ He disappears from frame but quickly reenters.

*Oberon* Wake when some vile thing is near.

⟶ He kisses her, almost a little wistful, and is gone.

# CROSSROADS

*Night* ⟶ A nymph and a fawn are locked in a steamy embrace. A noise interrupts them. They dive into the bushes and out of sight.

HERMIA, out of breath, the skirt of her dress shredded by briers, battles her bike through the thick foliage. She emerges into a clear-ing, catching up with a perplexed LYSANDER.

*Lysander* Fair love, you faint with wand'ring in the wood;
And to speak troth, I have forgot our way.

⟶ He looks at her, a little abashed. But she smiles at him. The smile becomes a laugh; the laugh becomes a long, but chaste kiss.

*Lysander* (cont.) We'll rest us, Hermia, if you think it good,
And tarry for the comfort of the day.

*Hermia* Be't so, Lysander.

⟶ She wanders in an exhausted trance into a sheltered area in the rocky wall. He watches her go, a little disappointed.

*Hermia* Find you out a bed;

Titania,
Queen of the
Fairies, and
her entourage
of female
fairies.

For I upon this bank will rest my head.

⌐ Five minutes later …

# CLEARING

*Night* ⌐ LYSANDER takes off his coat and rolls it into a pillow. He studies the contents of his saddlebag spread out around him—razor, hairbrush, shaving brush, and cream. He lies down, looks restlessly at the place HERMIA sleeps.

Meanwhile in her makeshift bedroom, HERMIA has removed her wet dress and her mud-fringed petticoats. She works in her low-cut bodice to fashion a soft bed from her clothing.

Moments later…

# CLEARING

*Night* ⌐ Close on HERMIA asleep. She opens her eyes to find a hand resting gently, if emphatically, on her breast. She rolls quickly over to find LYSANDER beside her.

*Lysander* One turf shall serve as pillow
  for us both,
One heart, one bed, two bosoms, and one troth.

*Hermia* Nay, good Lysander. For my
  sake, my dear,
Lie further off yet, do not lie so near.

⌐ LYSANDER, hoping *no* might not mean *no*, rolls up on top of her. It is only in this position he is revealed to be completely

*"Classical mythology always remained an important point of reference. What creatures people the primeval forests of Italy if not the nymphs, satyrs, sphinxes, and centaurs of Ovid's Metamorphoses."*
—*Michael Hoffman, Director*

naked. HERMIA is too shocked to speak.

*Lysander*  O, take the sense, sweet,
of my innocence!
I mean, that my heart unto yours is knit,
So that but one heart we can make of it.

⤙ LYSANDER goes to work on her
neck, hoping his kisses will complement
his argument.

*Lysander*  Two bosoms interchained
with an oath,
So then, two bosoms and a single troth.
Then by your side no bed-room me deny,
For lying so, Hermia, I do not lie.

*Hermia* (*smiles*)  Lysander riddles very
prettily.

⤙ She kisses him, then having lulled
him into a false sense of security, slips out
from under him and scoots away, picking
up a petticoat to cover herself.

*Hermia*  But, gentle friend, for love and
courtesy
Lie further off.

⤙ She throws him a petticoat to cover
himself.

*Hermia*  In human modesty.
Such separation as may well be said
Becomes a virtuous bachelor and a maid.

⤙ LYSANDER tries to protest. HERMIA's hand
flies up.

*Hermia*  So far be distant; and, good
night, sweet friend.
Thy love ne'er alter till thy sweet life end.

⤙ The virtuous bachelor wraps the
petticoat 'round him and heads back
down the hill.

*Lysander*  Amen, amen, to that fair
prayer, say I,
And then end life when I end loyalty!

⤙ He plops down, the petticoat still
around him.

*Lysander*  Here is my bed. Sleep give
thee all his rest!

*Hermia* (o.s.)  With half that wish the
wisher's eyes be pressed!

# CLEARING

*Later*  ⤙ HERMIA and LYSANDER
fitfully sleep. A strange crunching, something
approaches.

Close on PUCK, who seems to float low
through the undergrowth.

*Puck*  Through the forest have I gone,
But Athenian found I none,
On whose eyes I might approve
This flower's force in stirring love.

⤙ He emerges into the clearing on the
back of a huge turtle. He is the image of the
little Bacchus we saw in THESEUS' garden.
He looks all around. Nothing but . . .

*Puck*  Night and silence.
But wait . . .

—Who is here?

⤙ He goes close to LYSANDER.

*Oberon and Titania in the forest.*

*Puck*  Weeds of Athens he doth wear:
This is he, my master said,
Despised the Athenian maid.

↝ He spots the bike. From his approach, we know he's not seen anything like it before. He kicks at the tires, honks the horn. He climbs on and starts to ride. This is traveling. He heads across the open space to HERMIA's little bed.

*Puck*  And here the maiden, sleeping sound,
On the dank and dirty ground.
Pretty soul! She durst not lie.

↝ And back toward LYSANDER.

*Puck*  Near this lack-love, this kill-courtesy.

↝ Circling LYSANDER.

*Puck*  Churl, upon thy eyes I throw
All the power this charm doth owe.
When thou wak'st, let love forbid
Sleep his seat on thy eyelid.

↝ Leaning from the bike like a seasoned circus performer, he squeezes a drop of the magic liquid directly into LYSANDER's eye.

*Puck*  So awake when I am gone,
For I must now to Oberon.

↝ He pedals out of the shot. Almost immediately, DEMETRIUS enters.

*Demetrius*  I charge thee, hence, and do not haunt me thus.

↝ He flies by and out of shot as HELENA appears battling a flat tire. She rolls to a stop, exhausted.

*Helena*  O, wilt thou darkling leave me? Do not so.

*Demetrius* (o.s.)  Stay, on thy peril! I alone will go.

↝ HELENA throws her useless bike to the ground. She mutters to herself like a tennis player losing a match.

*Helena*  O, I am out of breath in this fond chase!
The more my prayer, the lesser is my grace.
Happy is Hermia, wheresoe'er she lies,
For she hath blessed and attractive eyes.

↝ She sits on the turtle. It moves slowly but she is too distracted to notice.

*Helena*  How came her eyes so bright? Not with salt tears.
If so, my eyes are oft'ner washed than hers.

↝ She falls off the turtle, gets up, and watches it go.

*Helena*  No, no, I am as ugly as a bear,
For beasts that meet me run away for fear.

↝ Not exactly running but . . . She sits down and, unconsciously, grabs at LYSANDER's petticoat to dry her tears and blow her nose. A man's leg . . . this she notices.

*Helena*  Lysander.

↝ No blood. No wound. She kneels beside him.

*Helena*  Lysander, if you live, good sir, awake.

↝ LYSANDER opens his eyes and beholds divinity.

*Lysander* (rising)  And run through fire I will for thy sweet sake.

*Hermia and her lover, Lysander, share a moment in the forest after their escape.*

⟶ She looks down at his nakedness. He grabs the petticoat and rewraps it.

*Lysander* Where is Demetrius? O, how fit a word
Is that vile name to perish on my sword!

*Helena* Do not say so, Lysander, say not so.
What though he love your Hermia? Lord, what though?
Yet Hermia still loves you. Then be content.

*Lysander* Content with Hermia! No; I do repent
The tedious minutes I with her have spent.
Not Hermia but Helena I love:
Who will not change a raven for a dove?

*Helena* Wherefore was I to this keen mockery born?

⟶ She slaps LYSANDER.

*Helena* When at your hands did I deserve this scorn?

⟶ He smiles at her, so she slaps him again.

*Helena* Is't not enough, is't not enough, young man,
That I did never, no, nor never can,
Deserve a sweet look from Demetrius' eye,
But you must flout my insufficiency?

⟶ Pulling herself together, she wipes her tears and marches to HERMIA's bike (hers being flat and PUCK having taken LYSANDER's).

*Helena* (*cont.*) But fare you well. Perforce I must confess

I thought you lord of more true gentleness.

⟶ She rides sadly away right past HERMIA's boudoir. LYSANDER watches anxiously but . . .

*Lysander* She sees not Hermia.

⟶ He grabs her broken-down bike and rides into the trees. He takes a turn around her.

*Lysander* Hermia, sleep thou there,
And never mayst thou come Lysander near!
And, all my powers, address your love and might
To honor Helen and to be her knight.

⟶ This last as he pedals limpingly away, his pettiskirt billowing behind.

# CLEARING

*Night* ⟶ HERMIA sleeps alone. The camera cranes down and pushes in over her face, closer, closer. Suddenly, she sits up and screams.

*Hermia* Ay me, for the pity! What a dream was here!

⟶ She climbs to her feet.

*Hermia* (*cont.*) Lysander, look how I do quake with fear.

⟶ She adds a petticoat to her bodice before leaving the safety of the niche.

*Hermia* (*cont.*) Lysander.

⟶ But he is gone. How can her LYSANDER be gone?

*Helena enters the forest in pursuit of Demetrius.*

*Lysander declares his love for Helena once the spell has been cast.*

"As long as people are being born and having children, and falling in love and getting married, and dying, then Shakespeare is relevant."
—Calista Flockhart

# TITANIA'S BOWER

*Night* — High in the treetops, the FAIRY QUEEN lies dreaming. Clatter and chat from below. Craning down we see dashing out of bushes, PUCK's enchanted boar, the orange and yellow skullcap still tied around its head.

The pig runs for the safety of the brambles as our troupe of actors emerge one by one, torches in hand. SNOUT pulls his cart behind him, now filled with rehearsal props and costumes. STARVELING's little dog barks at his feet. PETER QUINCE surveys the clearing, the ruin. It is like a natural amphitheater. There is sufficient moonlight for their work to be done.

*Quince* Here's a marvail's convenient place for our rehearsal.

— He steps off sufficient space for a stage, directing SNOUT to place the torches at regular intervals. STARVELING hands down costumes and props to FLUTE. The dog gets in a game of tug-of-war with SNUG over a makeshift lion's head.

BOTTOM leans against the cart, poring over the script, trying his best to look like Henry Irving.

*Bottom* Peter Quince?

*Quince* What sayest thou, bully Bottom?

*Bottom* (*shaking his head*) There are things in this comedy of Pyramus and Thisby that will never please. First, Pyramus must draw a sword to kill himself; which the ladies cannot abide.

*Lysander takes off in pursuit of Helena once the spell has been cast.*

"For my character, the journey starts with infatuation and an idea of romantic love, that he loves Hermia. Then they go into the woods and his darker side is revealed when the fairies put drugs on his eyes. Then he—I—fall in love with my lover's best friend, as so often happens, and I romp around with her for a bit. But she rejects me, and then when I wake up after the dream, this midsummer dream, I fall back in love with the right person. But I've learned something on the way."
—Dominick West

SNOUT hesitates in lighting another torch.

**Snout** By'r lakin, a parlous fear.

**Starveling** I believe we must leave the killing out,
when all is done.

QUINCE is deeply troubled. "Leave the killing out?" A general sense of paralysis. STARVELING stops unloading the cart. SNUG lets the dog have his ruff. Suddenly BOTTOM smacks the cart, startling them all.

**Bottom** Write me a prologue, and let the prologue seem to
say, we will do no harm with our swords, and that
Pyramus is not killed indeed; and, for the more
better assurance, tell them that I Pyramus am not
Pyramus, but Bottom the weaver. This will put them out of fear.

General relief.

**Quince** Well, we will have such a prologue. But there is two
hard things; that is, to bring the moonlight into a
chamber; for, you know, Pyramus and Thisby meet by moonlight.

A tougher problem. You can't write your way out of this one. BOTTOM looks up at the sky. There above him shines the round full moon.

**Bottom** Doth the moon shine that night we play our play?

**Quince** A calendar, a calendar! Look in the almanac;
find out moonshine, find out moonshine.

SNOUT goes tearing through his cart. QUINCE, FLUTE, and STARVELING help. All attention is on the hunt for the almanac except SNUG. He pulls a small book from inside his jacket, opens it and walks a little away.

**Snug** It doth shine that night.

But they don't hear him.

**Snug** (cont., louder) It doth shine that night.

BOTTOM takes a look, "In fact."

**Bottom** Why, then may you leave a casement of the
great chamber open, and the moon may shine in at the casement.

BOTTOM looks at QUINCE. "Next?"

**Quince** We must have a wall in the great chamber, for
Pyramus and Thisby, says the story, did talk through
the chink of a wall.

SNOUT and SNUG look at each other. They missed that. FLUTE checks his script, nods.

**Snout** You can never bring in a wall.

**Flute** What say you, Bottom?

BOTTOM, who is now engaged in working out his first entrance, scarcely looks up.

**Bottom** Some man or other must present Wall: and let him
hold his fingers . . .

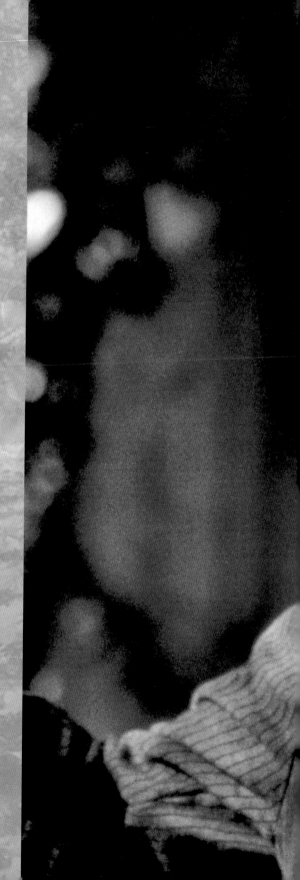

*Bottom rehearses his lines.*

⟶ He's very precise about this.

*Bottom* (cont.) . . . thus, and through
    that . . . cranny shall
Pyramus and Thisby whisper.

*Quince* Then all is well.

⟶ He says as the devil PUCK trundles up
the hill on HERMIA's bike.

*Puck* What hempen homespuns have we
    swagg'ring here,
So near the cradle of the Fairy Queen?

⟶ From his wide shot POV the actors
move to their places.

*Quince* Pyramus, you begin. When you
    have spoken your
speech, enter into that brake.

⟶ Cutting down among them—

*Quince* Speak, Pyramus. Thisby, stand forth.

⟶ FLUTE does awkwardly, clumsily.
PYRAMUS enters, very grand.

*Pyramus* [*Bottom*] Thisby, the
    flowers of odious savors sweet—

*Quince* Odors, odors.

*Pyramus* [*Bottom*] —odors savors
    sweet:
So hath thy breath, my dearest Thisby dear.
But hark, a voice! Stay thou but here awhile,
And by and by I will to thee appear.

⟶ BOTTOM pivots flamboyantly and
marches through a broken arch in the wall,
into a stand of trees that is "backstage." Up on
the ridge . . .

**Puck** A stranger Pyramus than e'er played here!

⟶ He coasts down the hill and in amongst the same trees, unseen.

**Flute** Must I speak now?

⟶ QUINCE looks up from making notations in his script.

**Quince** Ay, marry, must you. For you must understand
he goes but to see a noise that he heard,
and is to come again.

**Thisby [Flute]** Most radiant Pyramus, most lily-white of hue.

⟶ As THISBY/FLUTE continues, we cut "backstage" among the trees to find BOTTOM contemplating an elegant top hat and a walking stick laid out on a stump. BOTTOM cannot resist trying them on. PUCK, who stands nearby (but to whom BOTTOM is oblivious), blows gently in his direction, then again, on the surface of the stump. It becomes a shimmering mirror. BOTTOM, already in the throes of a burgeoning enchantment, gazes unquestioningly at his image. He is infatuated. Meanwhile on stage:

**Thisby [Flute]** As true as truest horse, that
yet would never tire,
I'll meet thee, Pyramus, at
Ninny's tomb.

**Quince** That's "Ninus' tomb," man.

⟶ He is on his feet, annoyedly approaching FLUTE. He points to the script.

**Quince** Why, you must not speak that yet. That you answer
to Pyramus. You speak all your part at once, cues
and all.

⟶ As he heads back to his prompt stool...

**Quince** Pyramus enter.

⟶ Backstage: BOTTOM responds; tries to remove the hat and glasses. He can't. He pulls at the hat again.

**Quince** (o.s.) Your cue is past; it is "never tire."

⟶ BOTTOM gives one final tug. The hat rises up to reveal a pair of enormous furry brown ears. He goes to enter. Angle in the faces of SNUG, SNOUT, and STARVELING.

**Bottom** (o.s.) If I were fair, Thisby, I were only thine.

⟶ Amazement. QUINCE backs away, stumbles over his stool.

**Quince** O monstrous! O strange!

⟶ Very strange. BOTTOM has sprouted ears. Hair has begun to grow on his cheeks and arms. He is still very recognizable as BOTTOM. He takes the glasses from his nose, thinking that might be the cause of all the fuss.

**Quince** Fly, masters!

**Starveling** We are haunted.

⟶ STARVELING and SNUG run for the woods. SNOUT begins to run tentatively

*Titania, Queen of the Fairies.*

Bottom as
Titania's new
paramour.

toward the stage to try and rescue his tinker's cart. As he inches forward:

**Snout** O Bottom, thou art changed! What do I see on thee?

**Bottom** What do you see? You see an ass head of your own, do you?

⟿ BOTTOM takes a step toward SNOUT, who abandons all hope and flees for safety. Meanwhile, QUINCE has snuck around the back of BOTTOM to rescue his stack of scripts, as BOTTOM turns.

**Quince** Bless thee, Bottom! Bless thee! Thou art translated.

⟿ QUINCE backs sadly away, turns, and hurries into the darkness. BOTTOM stares after them in wonder.

**Bottom** This is knavery of them to make me afeard.
This is to make an ass of me; to fright me, if they could.
But I will not stir from this place, do what they can and I
will sing, that they shall hear I am not afraid.

⟿ And he begins to sing.

**Bottom** The woosel cock so black of hue,
With orange-tawny bill,
The throstle with his note so true,
The wren with little quill—

# TITANIA'S BOWER

**Night** ⟿ Angle on: the sleeping TITANIA, who begins to coo and stir.

**Titania** What angel wakes me from my flow'ry bed?
On the ground.

**Bottom** The finch, the sparrow, and the lark,
The plain-song cuckoo gray,
Whose note full many man doth mark
And dares not answer NAAAYY.

⟿ TITANIA's head pops over the side of her bed at this very asslike bray.

**Titania** I pray thee, gentle mortal, sing again:
Mine ear is much enamored of thy note;
So is mine eye enthralled to thy shape;
And thy fair virtue's force perforce doth move me
On the first view to say, to swear, I love thee.

⟿ BOTTOM looks up into the trees at the lovesick queen, a little flattered, a little forcedly modest.

**Bottom** Methinks, mistress, you should have little
reason for that. And yet, to say the truth, reason and love keep little company together nowadays.

**Titania** Thou art as wise as thou art beautiful.

**Bottom** Not so, neither.

⟿ He begins to notice fairies and forest things creeping out of the trees to evaluate him, the cart, the bike, the costumes (like the munchkins when Dorothy lands in Oz).

*Bottom* ... but if I had wit enough to get out of this wood, I have enough to serve mine own turn.

*Titania* Out of this wood do not desire to go!

⟶ With impossible speed, the vines, the plants, form themselves into ropes, wrap themselves around BOTTOM's ankle and spring their own trap.

He ends up suspended upside down just above the level of TITANIA's bed.

*Titania* Thou shalt remain here, whether thou wilt or no.

⟶ She wraps her arms around his large head, caresses his ears.

*Titania* I am a spirit of no common rate. The summer still doth tend upon my state; And I do love thee. Therefore, go with me.

⟶ She signals a fairy in the trees above her to cut the rope that holds BOTTOM suspended. He falls into her bed. Before he can get up, she rolls on top of him, pressing him down into the flowers.

*Titania* I'll give thee fairies to attend on thee,
And they shall fetch thee jewels from the deep,
And sing, while thou on pressed flowers dost sleep:
And I will purge thy mortal grossness so,
That thou shalt like an airy spirit go.

⟶ BOTTOM is entranced.

*Titania* Peaseblossom! Cobweb! Moth! And Mustardseed!

*Bottom and Titania in the forest.*

These beautiful creatures (the wood nymphs from the fairy bar) appear at each corner of the bed.

*Peaseblossom*  Ready.

*Cobweb*  And I.

*Moth*  And I.

*Mustardseed*  And I.

All this beauty at his service. BOTTOM can't contain himself. He lets out a tremendous bray. They look at their lovestruck QUEEN, at each other. "I guess she knows what she's doing."

*Fairies*  Where shall we go?

# CLEARING

*Later*  The denizens of the fairy kingdom (TITANIA's supporters at least) are assembled for an al fresco feast. Many are dressed in pieces from the costume cart. Spread out on the rocks, the best of fairy country cooking. BOTTOM and TITANIA sit garlanded 'round with laurel leaves. The wine flows freely.

A group of grotesque little creatures dressed in the Victorian fashion of THESEUS' world burlesque the customs of the court. All assembled find this side-splittingly funny.

A pair of nymphs in the audience notice a couple of handsome satyrs lurking in the undergrowth behind them. A bit of surreptitious flirting ensues.

TITANIA kisses BOTTOM's nose, his forehead. She lifts an earthen jug and pours him a bowl of some kind of ruby red wine. In his eyes we see he is falling in love with her. She stands and lifts her glass to her new paramour.

*Titania*  Be kind and courteous to this gentleman;
Hop in his walks, and gambol in his eyes;
Feed him with apricocks and dewberries,
With purple grapes, green figs, and mulberries;
Nod to him, elves, and do him courtesies.
Hail mortal.

COBWEB and PEASEBLOSSOM lift their glasses.

*Fairies*  Hail, mortal!

*Other fairies*  Hail! Hail! Hail!

BOTTOM is amazed and moved at the great honor done him. He rises, lifts his glass in return.

*Bottom*  I cry your worship's mercy, heartily.

The assembled company applauds him. TITANIA takes a leafy crown all in gold and places it on BOTTOM's head. BOTTOM looks deeply into TITANIA's loving gaze. A tear comes to his eye.

The THREE FATES, now middle-aged, continue their endless task.

# TENT

*Later* → A small tented enclosure. BOTTOM is being prepared for a night of love by the QUEEN's attendants, supervised by COBWEB and PEASEBLOSSOM. All the attention makes him nervous.

*Bottom* I beseech your worship's name.

*Cobweb* (no nonsense) Cobweb. A little levity perhaps.

*Bottom* I shall desire you of more
  acquaintance,
good Master Cobweb: if I cut my finger, I
  shall make bold with you. Your name,
  honest gentleman?

→ They lift the crown long enough to place a band of little bells across his donkey forehead.

*Peaseblossom* Peaseblossom.

*Bottom* I pray you commend me to
  Mistress Squash,
your mother, and to Master Peascod, your father.

→ Nobody laughs. BOTTOM clears his throat as PEASEBLOSSOM fixes a bell-spangled belt around his waist.

*Bottom* Good Master Peasblossom I shall
  desire you of more
acquaintance too.

→ MOTH and MUSTARDSEED appear at the door, his escort. BOTTOM asks for the mirror one more time. He nods and walks out into . . .

# CLEARING

*Night* → A festival of fire and light. BOTTOM's little tent glows but its radiance is overmatched by the illuminated silks bedecking TITANIA's bed. As he walks forward, fairies strew his path with flowers.

*Titania* (o.s.) Come, lead him to my
  bower.

→ BOTTOM looks up to see the FAIRY QUEEN standing before her bed, her nakedness covered only by her long hair.

She descends the stair to meet him. Taking his hairy hand, she places it on her milk-white breast. They look deep into each other's eyes.

*Titania* The moon methinks looks with a
  wat'ry eye;
And when she weeps, weeps every little
  flower,
Lamenting some enforced chastity.

→ She embraces him then, surprised by something, steps away and looks down. BOTTOM looks down. The assembled FAIRIES look down—all at the area of BOTTOM's privates. They are all (as HERMIA says) amazed and know not what to say. TITANIA laughs with fascinated delight.

*Bottom* Hee-Haw!

→ A huge laugh runs through the fairy throng. TITANIA takes COBWEB aside.

*Titania* Tie up my lover's tongue, bring him silently.

⤳ Dissolve to:

# TITANIA'S BED

⤳ She rolls on top of her soft donkey love. She throws back her head in ecstasy. As she moans, we hear . . .

*Oberon* (*v.o.*) I wonder if Titania be awaked.

# CROSSROADS

*Night* ⤳ OBERON sits alone on his throne eating grapes beside his pet sphynxes.

*Oberon* Then what it was that next came in her eye,
Which she must dote on in extremity.

⤳ We hear a distant, happy hee-haw, the jingling of little bells. OBERON takes note. The donkeys are up early.

He sighs, and lowers his hand to stroke a sphynx's head. He jerks back. PUCK, a devilish grin on his face, sits in its place.

*Oberon* How now, mad spirit!
What night-rule now about this haunted grove?

*Puck* My mistress with a monster is in love.
⤳ He leans in close and whispers to OBERON. OBERON begins to laugh and laugh— a laugh that fills the entire forest.

*Oberon* This falls out better than I could devise.
But hast thou yet latched the Athenian's eyes
With the love juice, as I did bid thee do?

*Puck* I took him sleeping—that is finished too—

⤳ OBERON grabs PUCK's face, plants a big kiss on his forehead. PUCK purrs with pleasure, having pleased his master so. A noise in the underbrush—

*Oberon* Stand close: this is the same Athenian.

⤳ Half-clothed HERMIA passes underneath the tree followed by DEMETRIUS and his bike.

*Puck* This is the woman, but not this the man.

⤳ OBERON goes to backhand him. PUCK cringes.

# ON THE GROUND

*Hermia* Now I but chide; but I should use thee worse,
For thou, I fear, hast given me cause to curse.
If thou hast slain Lysander in his sleep,
Being o'er shoes in blood, plunge in the deep,
And kill me too.
It cannot be but thou has murd'red him
So should a murderer look, so dead, so grim.

⤳ In her frustruation, she throws the bike aside. Her face is flushed. She is breathing hard.

**Demetrius**  You spend your passion on a misprised mood:
I am not guilty of Lysander's blood.

**Hermia**  I pray thee, tell me then that he is well.

**Demetrius**  An if I could, what should I get therefore?

⌐ HERMIA suddenly realizes her [Lysander's] coat has come open to reveal her heaving bosom. DEMETRIUS can't help but stare. She flushes even redder.

**Hermia**  A privilege, never to see me more.

⌐ She slaps him hard in the face. Then throwing the coat around her, runs into the wood. DEMETRIUS watches her go.

**Demetrius**  There is no following her in this fierce vein.
Here therefore for a while I will remain.

⌐ He leans his bike on its kickstand. He takes off his coat and vest to fashion a bed for himself while . . .

# UP IN A TREE

**Oberon**  What hast thou done? Thou hast mistaken quite,
And laid the love juice on some true-love's sight.

⌐ PUCK expects the worst. OBERON speaks slowly, every word dripping with condescension.

**Oberon**  About the woods . . .

⌐ PUCK pulls out his notebook. OBERON takes it, smacks him on the head with it, hands it back.

**Oberon**  About the woods go swifter than the wind,
And *Helena of Athens* look thou find.

⌐ "Helena of Athens." He's got it.

**Oberon**  By some illusion see thou bring her here.
I'll charm his eyes against she do appear.

⌐ PUCK meanwhile has purloined another bike—no hands.

**Puck**  I go, I go; look how I go,
Swifter than arrow from the Tartar's bow.

⌐ He crashes off through the bushes. On the sleeping DEMETRIUS. OBERON leans in and whispers close in his ear.

**Oberon**  Flower of this purple dye,
Hit with Cupid's archery,
Sink in apple of his eye.
When his love he doth espy,
Let her shine as gloriously
As the Venus of the sky.
When thou ask'st, if she be by,
Beg of her for remedy.

⌐ PUCK races back into the clearing.

**Puck**  Captain of our fairy band,
Helena is here at hand;
And the youth, mistook by me,
Pleading for a lover's fee.
Shall we their fond pageant see?

*And directly to camera:*

*Puck* Lord, what fools these mortals be!

*LYSANDER still in his petticoat and very emotional, crashes after HELENA through the thick foliage.*

*Lysander* Why should you think that I should woo in scorn?

*He trips over a small log.*

*Lysander* Scorn and derision never come in tears.

*He falls again. Cutting out we see PUCK conducting two dwarfish henchmen holding either end of the offending log. The two of them move parallel to LYSANDER, awaiting the next opportunity.*

*Lysander* Look, when I vow, I weep;
and vows so born,
In their nativity all truth appears.
How can these things in me seem scorn to you,
Bearing the badge of faith, to prove them true?

*He goes down a third time, falls sprawling into the clearing.*

*Angle on: PUCK—it's like shooting fish in a barrel.*

*Helena* You do advance your cunning more and more.
When truth kills truth, O devilish-holy fray!
These vows are Hermia's: will you give her o'er?
Weigh oath with oath, and you will nothing weigh.

*Lysander* I had no judgment when to her I swore.

*Helena* Nor none, in my mind, now you give her o'er.

*She continues to back away from him. DEMETRIUS begins to stir.*

*Lysander* Demetrius loves her, and he loves not you.

*DEMETRIUS, over whom HELENA now directly stands. He sits up almost underneath her. She turns. He looks, and when he sees her, he loves.*

*Demetrius* O Helen, goddess, nymph, perfect, divine!
To what, my love, shall I compare thine eyne?

*He clutches at her skirt.*

*Demetrius* Crystal is muddy. O, how ripe in show
Thy lips, those kissing cherries, tempting grow!

*HELENA looks from one besotted suitor to the other.*

*Helena* O spite! O hell! I see you all are bent
To set against me for your merriment.

*She climbs onto her bike.*

*Helena* (cont.) Can you not hate me, as I know you do,
But you must join in souls to mock me too?

*Breaking into tears, she rides off down an adjacent path. The boys run after her.*

*PUCK laughs as they go.*

*Thwack—a walnut strikes him on the head. An annoyed OBERON gestures for him to follow.*

*Demetrius declares his love for Helena, after the spell has been cast.*

# DEEPER IN THE WOODS

HELENA fights to stay ahead. She's aided by the boys' incessant arguing.

**Lysander** And here, with all good will, with all my heart,
In Hermia's love I yield you up my part;
And yours of Helena to me bequeath,
Whom I do love, and will do till my death.

**Helena** (*over her shoulder*) Never did mockers waste more idle breath.

**Demetrius** Lysander, keep thy Hermia; I will none.
If e'er I loved her, all that love is gone.

**Lysander** Helen, it is not so.

At that moment, HERMIA appears from over a low cliff. HELENA swerves to miss her.

**Hermia** Lysander!

But he runs past her like she isn't there. She chases after him.

**Hermia** Lysander, love. (*beat*)
Why unkindly didst thou leave me so?

**Lysander** Why should he stay, whom love doth press to go?

He stops, confronts her.

**Lysander** Why seek'st thou me? Could not this make thee know,
The hate I bare thee made me leave thee so?

**Hermia** You speak not as you think: it cannot be.

Demetrius and Lysander fight for Helena.

⌐HELENA has stopped at a high point on the path.

From her POV: LYSANDER and HERMIA deep in conversation.

*Helena*  Lo, she is one of this confederacy!

⌐Outraged by the betrayal, she turns her bike and coasts toward the others.

*Helena*  Injurious Hermia! Most
    ungrateful maid!
Have you conspired, have you with *these*
    contrived
To bait me with this foul derision?

⌐HERMIA is completely nonplussed.

*Helena*  Is all the counsel that we two
    have shared,
The sister's vows, the hours that we have spent,
When we have chid the hasty-footed time
For parting us—O, is all forgot?
And will you rent our ancient love asunder
to join with men in scorning your poor
    friend?
It is not friendly, 'tis not maidenly.

*Hermia*  I understand not what you mean
    by this.

⌐She looks over HELENA's shoulder at DEMETRIUS and LYSANDER, who jostle with each other. Paranoid HELENA takes all this as fun at her expense.

*Helena*  Ay, do! Persever, counterfeit sad
    looks,
Make mouths upon me when I turn my back.
If you have any pity, grace or manners,
You would not make me such an argument.

*Hermia fights with Helena once she learns that both Demetrius and Lysander now claim to love Helena.*

⌐ She marches to her bike, leaving HERMIA in shock.

*Helena*  But fare ye well. 'Tis partly my
  own fault,
Which death or absence soon shall remedy.

⌐ She begins to pedal—but goes nowhere.

Wider angle: DEMETRIUS and LYSANDER, to prevent her escape, have lifted either end of the bike off the ground.

*Helena*  O excellent!

*Lysander*  Helen, I love thee; by my life
  I do!

*Hermia*  Sweet, do not scorn her so.

*Demetrius*  I say I love thee more than
  he can do.

*Lysander*  If thou say so, withdraw and
  prove it too.

*Demetrius*  Quick, come!

⌐ He puts down his end of the bike, the front end. HELENA weeps and pedals, pedals and weeps, and goes nowhere (truly like an experience from a nightmare).

HERMIA runs 'round the back of the bike, fights with LYSANDER to free it.

*Hermia*  Lysander, where to tends all this?

*Lysander*  Hang off, thou cat, thou burr!
  Vile thing, let loose!
Or I will shake thee from me like a serpent!

*Hermia*  Do you not jest?

*Helena*  Yes, sooth; and so do you.

⌐ At this moment: HERMIA manages to loose LYSANDER's grip. HELENA's tire catches. She shoots out of frame. She flies by DEMETRIUS, almost running him down. The others give chase. HERMIA brings up the rear.

*Hermia*  Am not I Hermia?
I am as fair now as I was erewhile.
Why, then you left me—
In earnest, shall I say?

*Lysander*  And never did desire to see
  thee more.
Be certain, nothing truer. 'Tis no jest
That I do hate thee, and love Helena.

# MUD PUDDLE

*Night*  ⌐ Who, at this moment, is skidding to a halt, barely managing to avoid a *huge mud puddle* that sits at the base of the clearing.

HERMIA now arrives in the clearing. She looks at LYSANDER. "How can this be?" Then at HELENA. Her eyes narrow.

*Hermia*  O me! You juggler! You canker
  blossom!
You thief of love!

⌐ It takes HELENA a moment to realize that it is she who is the subject of HERMIA's displeasure.

*Hermia*  What, have you come by night
And stol'n my love's heart from him?

⌐ HELENA tries to approach but finds that one foot has become badly stuck in the mud.

*Helena*  Fine, i'faith!
Have you no modesty, no maiden shame,
No touch of bashfulness? What, will you tear
Impatient answers from my gentle tongue?
Fie! Fie! You counterfeit, you puppet, you!

*Hermia*  Puppet? Why so? Ay, that way
    goes the game.

⟿ She moves purposefully toward
HELENA, unaware of the thornbush that rips
away her last petticoat.

*Hermia*  And are you grown so high in
    his esteem,
Because I am so dwarfish and so low?
How low am I, thou painted maypole? Speak!
How low am I? I am not yet so low
But that my nails can reach unto thine eyes.

⟿ She lunges at HELENA, catching her
around the waist. The force carries them
both into the mud puddle. HERMIA is on her
in a flash.

*Helena*  I pray you, though you mock me,
    gentlemen,
Let her not hurt me.

⟿ The boys hurry to the edge of the muck.

*Helena*  You perhaps may think,
Because she is something lower than myself,
That I can match her.

*Hermia*  Lower! Hark, again!

⟿ HERMIA may not be, moment to
moment, such a drama queen as HELENA, but
once roused—she slams HELENA's face into
the mud.

Meanwhile the boys provide no help because
neither will let the other get near enough to
HELENA to be the hero.

*Helena* (*pleading*)  Good Hermia, do not
    be so bitter with me.
And now, so you will let me quiet go,
To Athens will I bear my folly back,
And follow you no further.

⟿ HELENA manages to twist around, looks
into her eyes.

*Helena*  Let me go.

⟿ HERMIA relents a little, roughly lets
her go.

*Helena*  You see how simple and how
    fond I am.

⟿ HERMIA gets off of her.

*Hermia*  Why, get you gone. Who is't
    that hinders you?

*Helena*  A foolish heart, that I leave here
    behind.

*Hermia* (*eyes blazing*)  What, with
    Lysander?

⟿ HELENA runs.

*Helena*  With Demetrius!

⟿ By the time HERMIA catches her again, she
is near enough to the bank that LYSANDER and
DEMETRIUS can each grab a hand. HERMIA, way
beyond reason, clings firmly to her skirt, trying
to drag her back. Tug-of-war. HELENA screams.

*Lysander*  Be not afraid. She shall not
    harm thee, Helena.

*Demetrius*  No, sir, she shall not, though
    you take her part.

    ⌒ He gives a strong pull—a ripping
sound, and HELENA comes free. HERMIA falls
backward holding her torn skirt.

*Helena*  She was a vixen when she went
    to school;
And though she be but little, she is fierce.

*Hermia*  "Little" again! Nothing but "low"
    and "little"!
Why will you suffer her to flout me thus?
Let me come to her.

    ⌒ She fights her way up the bank.
LYSANDER steps forward; she grabs at him.

*Lysander*  Get you gone, you dwarf.
You minimus, of hindering knot-grass made;
You bead, you acorn.

    ⌒ And throws her back in the mud.

*Lysander* (to Demetrius)  Now she holds
    me not.
Now follow, if thou dar'st, to try whose right,
Of thine or mine, is most in Helena.

    ⌒ DEMETRIUS looks at him.

*Demetrius*  Follow! Nay, I'll go with thee.
    Cheek by jowl.

    ⌒ HELENA watches them march into the
woods. HERMIA climbs up to the edge of the
pond. HELENA realizes she is without protection.

*Hermia* (under her breath)  You, mistress, all
    this coil is 'long of you.

    ⌒ HERMIA's expression changes. She smiles
at HELENA, holds out her hand for aid.

*Hermia* (cont.)  Nay, go not back.

    ⌒ HELENA takes a few steps forward,
hesitates.

*Helena*  I will not trust you, I,
Nor longer stay in your curst company.
Your hands than mine are quicker for a fray,
My legs are longer though, to run away.

    ⌒ She throws off her muddy petticoats
for better mobility and runs into the woods.
HERMIA tries to leap after her but loses her
footing and goes facedown in the slick mud.

Her head pops up; nothing but the whites of
her eyes. Then summoning up all remnants
of her dignity, she stands, collects herself.

*Hermia*  I am amazed, and know not
    what to say.

    ⌒ And walks off into the woods.

A long beat—nothing but an empty clearing,
a muddy puddle, moonlight and one lone
bicycle. From out of the muck rises up a
strange little froglike creature. He looks
around, "What was all that about?" and sinks
back into the mire.

*Oberon* (o.s.)  This is thy negligence.

# OBERON'S THRONE

    ⌒ OBERON grabs PUCK by the ears and
holds him suspended in the air. His ears
begin to stretch like something elastic.

*Oberon*  Still thou mistak'st,
Or else committ'st thy knaveries willfully.

"Bottom as the donkey presented a very specific problem in the film. In many productions the actor applies a mask that completely consumes him. Bottom, the man, goes away. Given the importance of his relationship with Titania, we could not afford to lose him. We needed an image that suggested an ass. It had to serve the comedy but remain somehow sensual. After much anxious searching, I found a small figure of Pan in a large Moreau canvas of Jupiter and Semele. Sensual, dreamy, bestial, beautiful; it became our model. Gabriella Pescucci, the designer, translated it into a sketch that emphasized its humanity. It was very ably executed by the talented hands of makeup artist Paul Engelen and hairdresser Carol Hemming."
—Michael Hoffman, Director

And on cue, fog creeps out of the forest behind them.

*Oberon* (*v.o.*) And lead these testy rivals so astray,
As one come not within another's way.

# OBERON'S THRONE

Back to: OBERON, who hands PUCK a vial.

*Oberon* Then crush this herb into
Lysander's eye.
Whiles I in this affair do thee employ,
I'll to my queen and beg her Indian boy;
And then I will her charmed eye release
From monster's view, and all things shall be
peace.

Smash cut to:

# ANOTHER PART OF THE FOREST

*Moments later* A thick dark cloud coming right at camera. It's PUCK, his bicycle trailing a heavy fog behind it.

*Puck* Up and down, up and down,
I will lead them up and down:
I am feared in field and town:
Goblin, lead them up and down.

LYSANDER and DEMETRIUS circle each other. LYSANDER takes the first swing but PUCK rides by. The befogged LYSANDER loses sight of his quarry.

*Lysander* Where art thou, proud Demetrius?

*Puck* Believe me, king of shadows, I mistook.
Did not you tell me I should know the man
By the Athenian garments he had on?

OBERON relents, snaps him back beside him. PUCK can't help but rub his ears.

*Oberon* Thou see'st these lovers seek a place to fight.

# ANOTHER PART OF THE FOREST

DEMETRIUS and LYSANDER fashion clubs from dangerous-looking branches.

*Oberon* (*v.o.*) Hie therefore, Robin, overcast the night.
The starry welkin cover thou anon
With drooping fog, as black as Acheron.

PUCK calls out (in DEMETRIUS' voice) from the other side of the clearing.

*Puck* (o.s.) Here, villain. Where art thou?

*Lysander* I will be with thee straight.

LYSANDER runs in the direction of the voice, in time to avoid a powerful blow from DEMETRIUS' club.

*Demetrius* Lysander! Speak again!
Thou runaway, thou coward, art thou fled?

PUCK rides in circles around DEMETRIUS, enveloping him completely in the heavy mist.

*Puck [as Lysander]* Come recreant! Come, thou child.

*Demetrius* Yea, art thou there?

*Puck* Follow my voice. We'll try no manhood here.

DEMETRIUS chases him out as LYSANDER rushes in, out of breath.

*Lysander* The villain is much lighter-heeled than I.
I followed fast, but faster he did fly,
That fallen am I in dark uneven way,
And here will rest me.

LYSANDER lies down.

*Lysander* Come thou gentle day!

A short distance off DEMETRIUS thrashes in the fog.

*Puck [as Lysander]* Come hither.
I am here.

*Demetrius* Nay, then, thou mock'st me.

Thou shalt buy this dear,
If ever I thy face by daylight see.

He breathes deep of the fog. It hits him like a drug. He yawns.

*Demetrius* Now, go thy way. Faintness
constraineth me
To measure out my length on this cold bed.
By day's approach look to be visited.

# ANOTHER PART OF THE FOREST II

HERMIA, too, completely spent. She rocks back and forth on her heels, her arms wrapped 'round herself.

*Hermia* Never so weary, never so in woe:
I can no further crawl, no further go.

She collapses where she stands.

*Hermia* Here will I rest me till the break
of day.
Heavens shield Lysander, if they mean a fray!

# ANOTHER PART OF THE FOREST III

HELENA, lost, exhausted, can't see her hand in front of her face. Falling to her knees, she prays to any god that will listen.

*Helena* O weary night, O long and
tedious night,
Abate thy hours! Shine comforts from the east,
That I may back to Athens by daylight,
From these that my poor company detest:
And sleep, that sometimes shuts up sorrow's
eye,

Steal me awhile from mine own company.

⌒ Too tired even to cry, HELENA lies down on the ground.

# ANOTHER PART OF THE FOREST IV

⌒ A moment: nothing but fog in the moonlight. A great whirring sound and the fog begins to disperse. Close angles of wheels spinning rapidly. Pulling back we reveal the four bikes (in various states of disrepair) floating just above the ground; pedals turning madly. The fog is sucked back magically into the saddlebags.

The fog drifts away to reveal the four lovers not in four diverse places but lying all peacefully together. LYSANDER is magically closer to HERMIA, DEMETRIUS to HELENA. And they all lie together under the protection of an ancient weathered oak in a field now alive with red flowers. PUCK appears in the dying mist.

*Puck* On the ground
Sleep sound:
I'll apply
To . . .

⌒ He crouches next to DEMETRIUS, starts with the love juice . . . then moves to LYSANDER.

*Puck* . . . your eye,
Gentle lover, remedy.

⌒ He squeezes the drops into LYSANDER's eyelid.

*Puck* When thou wak'st,
Thou tak'st

True delight
In the sight
Of thy former lady's eye.

⌒ The sleeping LYSANDER whispers a word, a name—HERMIA.

*Puck* And the country proverb known
That every man should take his own,
In your waking shall be shown.

⌒ A noise in the distance. PUCK sees against the dawn sky the approach of an old wooden haywain drawn by a pair of white oxen.

As the cart passes us, there is PUCK magically reclining in the back.

*Puck* Jack shall have Jill;
Nought shall go ill;
The man shall have his mare again, and all
    shall be well.

# EDGE OF THE FOREST

*Dawn* ⌒ The cart emerges from the forest, heads down the widening path. And we crane up to reveal that this dense dark endless wood, this place of chaos and confusion, is in fact one of those strange little wooded topknots, limited, manageable, on the crown of a long cultivated Tuscan hill. On the rich laughter of PUCK we . . .

Cut to:

# TITANIA'S BOWER

⟿ The first glow of dawn. Exhausted fairies among the ruins. COBWEB and PEASEBLOSSOM lean against each other almost asleep.

*Titania* (o.s.) Come, sit thee down upon this flow'ry bed,
While I thy amiable cheeks do coy.

⟿ Pulling back we find BOTTOM and TITANIA nestling into the bed that now rests on the ruins' floor. She takes his head in her lap, feeding him the summer's first red grapes.

*Titania* (cont.) And stick musk roses in thy sleek smooth head,
And kiss thy fair large ears, my gentle joy.

⟿ She does, and it tickles and he bleats a little, and she can't help but laugh and he can't help but love her.

*Bottom* Where's Mounsieur Cobweb?

⟿ COBWEB opens one eye, moves reluctantly toward him. PEASEBLOSSOM smirks "better her than me" . . .

*Cobweb* Ready . . .

*Bottom* Scratch my head, good mounsieur.

⟿ Fairies begin to appear reluctantly around them. It's dawn. It's time they get off work, but their QUEEN seems ready to rave.

*Bottom* Where's Mounsieur Mustardseed?
Trying to make a surreptitious exit.

*Mustardseed* Ready . . .

*Bottom* Pray you, leave your curtsy, good mounsieur.

⟿ He nods—"Whatever."

*Mustardseed* What's you will?

*Bottom* Nothing, good mounsieur, but to heip Cavalery
Cobweb to scratch.

⟿ They scratch halfheartedly. COBWEB start to nod off. BOTTOM shares with TITANIA a little domestic intimacy.

*Bottom* I must to the barber's,
Methinks I am marvail's hairy
about the face; and I am such a tender ass, if my hair do but tickle me, I must scratch.

*Titania*
What, wilt thou hear some music, my sweet love?

⟿ The fairy band, in the act of putting their instruments away, freeze, dreading the reply.

*Titania* Or say, sweet love, what thou desirest to eat.

⟿ The nymphs whose job it is to clean up the nights repast stop in their tracks. BOTTOM surveys the country delicacies.

*Bottom* I could munch your good dry oats. Methinks I have great desire to a bottle of hay.

⟿ The satyrs look at each other—"Hay?"

*Bottom* Good hay, sweet hay, hath no
    fellow.

⟶ But this long and marvelous night has
taken its toll on him as well.

*Bottom* But, I pray you, let none of your
    people stir me:
I have an exposition of sleep come upon me.

⟶ She leads him the few steps to her
bed. Two very tired fairies go to work on
those infernal cranks and the bed rises into
the treetops.

*Titania* Sleep thou, and I will wind thee
    in my arms.
Fairies, be gone, and be all ways away.

⟶ They do not let the door hit them on
their fairy asses on the way out. But neither TITA-
NIA or BOTTOM mind at all. Nothing interferes
with their bliss. She wraps herself around him.

*Titania* So doth the woodbine the sweet
    honeysuckle
Gently entwist; the female ivy so
Enrings the barky fingers of the elm.
O, how I love thee!

*Bottom* (smiling) How I dote on thee!

⟶ As they drift off, the camera cranes
higher into the trees. There, OBERON watches
with mixed emotions; pleasure at the success of
his venture, colored by a melancholy wish that
his life with TITANIA might be so simple, so tender. PUCK's arrival interrupts his contemplation.

*Oberon* Welcome, good Robin. See'st
    thou this sweet sight?
Her dotage now I do begin to pity.

⟶ PUCK produces a piece of parchment, a
long list of signatures, marks and scratches.
"We the Undersigned of the Fairy Kingdom."
He reads it over.

*Oberon* I will undo this hateful imperfec-
    tion of her eyes.

⟶ He drops silently onto the bed. Very
near her now, he touches gently her face.

*Oberon* Be as thou wast wont to be;
See as thou wast wont to see.

⟶ He lets drop a single drop from a
white flower, the antidote, onto her eyelid.

*Oberon* Now, my Titania, wake you, my
    sweet Queen.

⟶ She opens her eyes. She looks deep into
OBERON, seems to see him anew, love him anew.

*Titania* My Oberon, what visions have I
    seen!
Methought I was enamored of an ass.

*Oberon* There lies your love.

⟶ TITANIA sees the sleeping BOTTOM and
recoils in shock from the very curious creature in her bed. She climbs into OBERON's
arms to be away from him.

*Titania* How came these things to pass?
O, how mine eyes do loathe his visage now.

*Titania awakens to Oberon, after he has removed the spell.*

⟶ She looks past OBERON to PUCK, who smiles behind him—suspiciously . . . Their eyes meet—war, peace, what's it to be?

*Oberon* (*a compromise*) Silence awhile.

⟶ He takes her in his strong arms. Their faces touch.

*Titania* Music, ho, music! Such as charmeth sleep!

*Oberon* Sound, music!

⟶ Below among the ruins, musicians begin to play. Panning away from them we find OBERON and TITANIA walking away arm and arm through the glade.

*Oberon* Now thou and I are new in amity.

⟶ Deep harmonic tones issue, it seems, from the earth itself as the FATES, now three very ancient women, having lived an entire lifetime in one night, continue their ceaseless weaving, measuring, their ceaseless cutting of thread.

# IN THE BRANCHES

⟶ PUCK crouches over BOTTOM.

*Puck* Now, when thou wak'st with thine own fool's eyes peep.

⟶ He squeezes into BOTTOM's eyes more than enough of the white stuff.

# FACE OF CLIFF

⟶ While the music plays we crane along the face of the cliff. Within the Etruscan tombs that dot it:

- Dwarves at a forge repair the lovers' battered bikes.
- Fairies restitch torn garments.
- Water nymphs wash out muddy petticoats.
- Satyrs fashion laurel crowns for the lovers' hair.

⟶ Finally we arrive on TITANIA and OBERON reclining on a simple bed. Their lips come together in a kiss until . . .

*Puck* Fairy King, attend, and mark:
I do hear the morning lark.

⟶ Indeed. And, too, the sound of distant baying hounds.

*Oberon* Then, my Queen, in silence sad,
Trip we after night's shade.
We the globe can compass soon.
Swifter than the wand'ring moon.

*Titania*  Come, my lord, and in our flight,
Tell me how it came this night,
That I sleeping here was found
With these mortals on the ground.

The KING and QUEEN smile at each other in
acknowledgment of their newfound affection as
their image fades to nothing. The impression of
their figures is left sculpted in the stone.

# VINEYARD

*Dawn* ⟶ A team of beaters tramples
through the underbrush. A wild boar (the
orange-capped wild boar) runs hell-bent through
a vineyard and into the trees. And after him
come the hunters, THESEUS, HIPPOLYTA, EGEUS,
and a party of well-turned-out courtiers.

THESEUS walks up beside HIPPOLYTA. He
indicates the knot of trees (the knot we've
seen before) at the top of the next hill.

*Theseus*  We will, fair Queen, up to the
    mountain's top,
And mark the musical confusion
Of hounds and echo in conjunction.

⟶ She does not respond. He bumbles
anxiously on.

*Theseus*  My hounds are bred out of the
    Spartan kind,
So flewed, so sanded; and their heads are
    hung
With ears . . .

⟶ She simply walks away. His yattering
has failed to impress.

# TUSCAN CLEARING

*Dawn* Up ahead: The dogs bay. The boar runs. The dogs pursue it through the trees and into the clearing. The hunters crash after them. They reach the place where the lovers sleep, the field of flowers, and would continue on were it not for HIPPOLYTA. She appears through the thick greenery. THESEUS, who has ridden past, returns.

*Hippolyta* But, soft! What nymphs are these?

⌐ Their POV. The four lovers, naked in the flowers, except for the laurel leaves in their hair. DEMETRIUS embraces HELENA; LYSANDER, HERMIA, and next to them their immaculately clean, immaculately folded clothing. Four pristine bicycles stand in a row, the morning sun glinting off their metalwork.

EGEUS walks into the clearing, stands beside the DUKE. Other courtiers arrive. An awkward silence. EGEUS' face is bright red. He whispers hoarsely, emphatically:

*Egeus* My lord, this is my daughter here asleep;
And this, Lysander; this Demetrius is;
This Helena, old Nedar's Helena:
I wonder of their being here together.

*Theseus* No doubt they rose up early to observe
The rite of May.

⌐ A few uncomfortable laughs.

*Theseus and Hippolyta discover the four young lovers in the morning once Puck has corrected the miscast spell.*

*Theseus* Go, bid the huntsmen wake
   them with their horns.

— Tight of horns. Tight of the
huntsmen's faces. The sound of brass
and baying dogs.

On the lovers: HELENA opens her eyes
first but seeing DEMETRIUS, feeling his
warm embrace, closes them again,
not wanting this dream to end.

*Theseus* (*unsmiling*) Good morrow,
   friends. Saint Valentine is past:
Begin these wood birds but to couple
   now?

— The lovers open their eyes, look
up at the hunting party silhouetted
against the sun. Suddenly one realizes, then
they all do, just how compromised they are.
A wild scramble for clothing, anything.

*Lysander* Pardon my lord.

*Theseus* I pray you all, stand up.

— They do. Holding an odd assortment
of mismatched clothing in front of them,
like paper dolls, leaving them vulnerable to
the rear.

*Theseus* (*cont.*) I know you two are rival
   enemies.
How comes this gentle concord in the world,
That hatred is so far from jealousy,
To sleep by hate, and fear no enmity?

*Lysander* My lord, I shall reply amazedly,
Half sleep, half waking: But, as I think
I came with Hermia hither. Our intent
Was to be gone from Athens, where we might

The four
young lovers.

Without
   the peril of the
   Athenian law—

— EGEUS has him dead to rights.

*Egeus* Enough, enough, my lord; you have
   enough.
I beg the law, the law, upon his head.
They would have stol'n away; they would,
   Demetrius,
Thereby to have defeated you and me,
You of your wife and me of my consent,
Of my consent that she should be your wife.

— Even now he will forgive DEMETRIUS if
he'll collude with him in his desire to control

his daughter. All eyes are on DEMETRIUS. We should wonder a little if he has it in him to challenge authority.

*Demetrius*  My good lord, I wot not by what power—
But by some power it is—my love to Hermia,
Melted as the snow.

⌐  EGEUS can't believe it. He looks around for some source of support.

*Demetrius*  And all the faith, the virtue of my heart,
The object and the pleasure of mine eye,
Is only Helena.

⌐  He gives her a modest kiss. THESEUS looks at this unlikely supplicant, at EGEUS. The entire court is watching him, awaiting his decision. The law is the law. He starts to speak, then stops. Signaling to HIPPOLYTA, he walks with her a little away. They lean together talking in low tones.

The lovers watch in anticipation. From their POV, HIPPOLYTA makes an impassioned point. THESEUS listens. They return to the anxious group.

*Theseus*  Fair lovers, you are fortunately met.
Egeus, I will overbear your will.

⌐  There is an audible gasp from the crowd. THESEUS smiles at HIPPOLYTA. He has chosen to put the law aside. The lovers can barely contain their joy, but their present state makes it difficult for them to express it.

*Theseus*  For in the temple, by and by, with us
These couple shall eternally be knit.

⌐  He gestures to the master of the hunt, who calls to the woodsmen, who sound the horns to call off the dogs.

*Theseus*  Away with us to Athens! Three and three,
we'll hold a feast in great solemnity.
come, Hippolyta.

⌐  With a smile to his bride and a wink at the lovers, he offers his arm to HIPPOLYTA. They walk together away. The others follow, joyful, except EGEUS. He looks back at DEMETRIUS, spits on the ground, and as he does, gets whacked in the head by a low branch.

Dissolve to:

# TITANIA'S BOWER

*Morning*  ⌐  Again the clearing is quiet. Up above, BOTTOM sleeps soundly. The ass head is still in place until (as PUCK said) he wakes.

Detail of: one of the cranks. It gives way. It spins.

The fairy bed is in free-fall. Down, down, smack.

# FOREST FLOOR

⟶ It hits the forest floor. A pause.

*Bottom*   When my cue comes, call me, and I will answer. My next is, "Most fair Pyramus."

⟶ His head pops up over the bed. He looks around, no longer the donkey-man but plain old NICK BOTTOM the weaver.

*Bottom* (cont.)   Heigh-ho! Peter Quince?

⟶ Nothing. He notices the prop chest, neatly packed and placed in SNOUT's cart.

*Bottom*   Flute, Snout the tinker?
     Starveling?
God's my life, stol'n hence, and left me asleep?

⟶ He momentarily feels something beneath him and looks down to discover a tiny nest in the shape of TITANIA's fairy bed. Inside, among the little feathers, is something even smaller in gold. It is the golden crown given him by the Fairy Queen, now no bigger than a thimble. He looks hard.

*Bottom*   I have had a most rare vision. I
     have had a dream,
past the wit of man to say what dream it was.
Man is but an ass, if he go about to expound
     this dream.

⟶ He hurries to the pond to study his reflection in the clear water.

*Bottom*   Methought I was—there is no
     man can tell what

methought I was— Methought I was—and
     methought I had—

⟶ He feels for the ears, like phantom limbs, he can still almost feel them. He takes a look at his crotch.

*Bottom*   But man is but a patched fool if
     he will offer to say what methought I had.

⟶ He leans against a nearby log and looks at the little golden crown in his hand.

*Bottom*   The eye of man hath not heard,
The ear of man hath not seen, man's hand is
     not
able to taste, his tongue to conceive, nor his
     heart
to report, what my dream was.

⟶ He is moved by the memory, the glory of it all, the adulation, but mostly the love.

# FOREST

*Day* ⟶ BOTTOM hauls SNOUT's cart through the woods.

*Bottom*
I will get Peter Quince to write a ballet of
     this dream. It shall be called "Bottom's
     Dream," because it hath no bottom.

⟶ And through the portal out of the fairy kingdom toward home. He looks again at his beautiful little gift. It seems to inspire him, raise his spirits. He puts it carefully in his pocket.

# TOWN SQUARE

*Day* — QUINCE, FLUTE, SNOUT, and STARVELING sit listless and defeated at the base of a huge stone well that marks the center of the piazza. It is lunchtime, but they are too depressed even to eat. Something strikes QUINCE.

*Quince* Have you sent to Bottom's house? Is he come home yet?

*Starveling* He cannot be heard of. Out of doubt he is transported.

— They sink back into despondency. Even STARVELING's dog is sad.

*Flute* If he come not, then the play is marred. It goes not forward, doth it?

— QUINCE and STARVELING look at him. "Duh."

*Snug* (o.s.) Masters:

— They're all once again hopeful at SNUG's approach. He shakes his head—more bad news.

*Snug* . . . the Duke is coming from the temple,
and there is two or three lords and ladies more married. If our sport had gone forward, we had all been made men.

— At this moment, MASTER ANTONIO parades his own troupe arrogantly across the square. FLUTE can contain himself no longer. He bursts into tears, real tears.

*Flute* O sweet bully Bottom! Thus hath he lost sixpence

a day during his life. And the Duke had not given him
sixpence a day for playing Pyramus, I'll be hanged.
He would have deserved it.

*Quince* (*nodding*) Sixpence a day in Pyramus, or nothing.

— That puts a period on it with nothing more to say. They rise one by one in the empty square and begin to disband. But as they start on their separate ways, there comes a familiar sound of bells. The bells, the clatter, the jingle of SNOUT's cart.

*Bottom* (o.s.) Where are these lads?

— He bursts through the gate at the far end of the square.

*Bottom* Where are these hearts?

— They race to meet him. QUINCE gets there first.

*Quince* Bottom! O most courageous day! O most happy hour!

— They crowd 'round him.

*Bottom* Masters, I am to discourse wonders.

*Quince* Let us hear, sweet Bottom.

*Bottom* I will tell you everything, right as it fell out, but if I tell you *now*, I am not true Athenian.

— They look quizzically at him.

*Bottom* All that I will tell you is, that the Duke hath dined.

*Bottom returns from his "night" in the forest.*

*(left to right) Demetrius, Helena, Lysander, and Hermia at their wedding banquet.*

～ The time. Their faces. Panic. There is
*no time!* BOTTOM gestures for calm.

*Bottom* Get your apparel together.

～ The actors prepare.

## MARKET SQUARE

～ SNOUT gives old STARVELING a shave
before the old mirror on his cart.

*Bottom* (*v.o.*) Good strings to your
   beards, new ribbons
to your pumps; every man look o'er his part.

## MARKET SQUARE

～ THISBY/FLUTE sashays very seriously
in a rehearsal skirt. QUINCE, equally somber,
evaluates.

*Bottom* Let Thisby have clean linen; and
   let not him that
plays the lion par his nails.

*Theseus and Hippolyta share a toast at their wedding banquet.*

## BOTTEGA

⌐ SNUG works at something we don't quite see; he puts a wooden wheel into place. Two little boys look in at the shop door. SNUG glowers at them. He roars. They roar back. He flinches.

## VILLA GATES

*Early evening* ⌐ The great gates of the palace open. The ragtag players look as sharp as their natures allow. BOTTOM, unapologetic in his white suit, is as dumb-struck as the rest of them by the grandeur of the place.

## FORMAL GARDEN

⌐ BOTTOM continues to whisper instruction as they are escorted by the officious PHILOSTRATE through the grounds.

*Bottom* And, most dear actors, eat no onions
no garlic, for we are to utter sweet breath, and I do not doubt but to hear them say it is a sweet comedy.

⌐ Suddenly BOTTOM stops in his tracks. The others watch him as he wanders off the path.

From their POV we see him enter the grotto. He is drawn irresistibly to the statue of the garlanded goddess. She holds in one hand an earthen jug, in the other a small bowl, very like one from which he'd drunk TITANIA's wine. He continues to stare but it is a love he can remember only through dense and dreamlike haze. He reaches out to touch the cool white marble.

*Philostrate* (o.s.) If it please you.

⟿ BOTTOM returns to his companions. They stare at him.

*Bottom* No more words. Away!

⟿ They do not move. They just watch him.

*Bottom* GO AWAY!

⟿ But he can't help but throw a look back over his shoulder.

# FORMAL GARDEN

*Night* ⟿ The end of the feast. THESEUS speaks with a group of his male friends. EGEUS sulks at his place, toying petulantly with his dessert. HIPPOLYTA is at the next table chatting with the lovers about their very odd experiences.

*Demetrius* These things seem small and indistinguishable,
Like far-off mountains turned into clouds.

*Helena* And I have found Demetrius like a jewel
Mine own, and not mine own.

⟿ HIPPOLYTA, touched by HELENA's deep joy, embraces her then moves along the table, accepting congratulations, to THESEUS. He turns from his companions to look into the eyes of his new wife.

*Hippolyta* 'Tis strange, my Theseus, that these lovers speak of.

*Theseus* More strange than true. I never may believe
These antique fables, nor these fairy toys.
Lovers and madmen have such seething brains,
Such shaping fantasies, that apprehend
More than cool reason ever comprehends.
Such tricks hath strong imagination,
That if it would but apprehend some joy,
It comprehends some bringer of the joy;
Or in the night, imagining some fear,
How easy is a bush supposed a bear!

*Hippolyta* But all the story of the night told over,
And all their minds transfigured so together,
More witnesseth than fancy's images,
And grows to something of great constancy;
But, howsoever, strange and admirable.

⟿ THESEUS smiles. There is something convincing in the curious consistency of the lovers' tales (and a wedding night is no time for an argument). Instead he stands and lifts his glass to the lovers.

*Theseus* Joy, gentle friends! Joy and fresh days of love
accompany your hearts!

⟿ All the diners rise. The sound of a hundred voices.

*All* Joy and fresh days of love.

⟿ Only EGEUS does not rise or speak. LYSANDER rises to answer the toast.

*Lysander*  More than to us
Wait in your royal walks, your board, your bed!

⟶ THESEUS and HIPPOLYTA smile. The diners applaud enthusiastically. LYSANDER smiles across at EGEUS, who very pointedly pushes back his chair and walks away. LYSANDER looks at HERMIA in awkward silence. THESEUS breaks it.

*Theseus*  Come now, what masques, what dances shall we have . . .

⟶ He throws an arm around each of his fellow newlyweds.

*Theseus*  To wear away this long age of *three hours*
Between our after-supper and bedtime?
Where is our usual manager of mirth?

⟶ PHILOSTRATE appears across the table from him.

*Philostrate*  Here, mighty Theseus.

*Theseus*  What revels are in hand? Is there no play,
To ease the anguish of a torturing hour?

*Philostrate*  There is a brief how many sports are ripe.

⟶ He hands THESEUS a document, a list.

Cut to:

# HOLDING AREA

⟶ Star search. An elaborate assortment of the best of the area's talent, a commedia dell'arte troupe practicing pratfalls, a fat soprano sings an aria from *Aida* while resting on a papier-mâché tiger. And an even fatter tenor in unlikely blackface prepares to strangle his Desdemona. Two men in armor joust on undersized stuffed horses.

*Theseus* (v.o.)  "The battle with the Centaurs, to be sung
By an Athenian eunuch to the harp."

⟶ His tortured voice cracks.

*Theseus* (v.o.)  We'll none of that.

⟶ Another company costumed for a Greek tragedy.

*Theseus* (v.o.)  "The riot of the tipsy Bacchanals,
Tearing the Thracian singer in their rage."

⟶ One of them, a little unsteady on his *cothurnus*, falls and almost knocks down a plaster column.

*Theseus* (v.o.)  That is an old device; and it was played
When I from Thebes came last a conqueror.

⟶ Next, MASTER ANTONIO and his company of prigs. He puts his actors, all dressed in short Roman tunics, through their paces, tapping out a rhythm with his walking stick. Theirs is a kind of stilted but well-rehearsed dramatic reading.

*Theseus* (v.o.)  "The thrice three Muses mourning for the death
Of Learning, late deceased in beggary."
That is some satire, keen and critical.

⟶ MASTER ANTONIO's contemptuous glance leads us to QUINCE, BOTTOM, et al.

*Snout plays the wall "Through which the lovers . . . Pyramus and Thisby, Did whisper often very secretly."*

BOTTOM is at work on his makeup. THISBY/FLUTE studies the actresses from the other companies, tries with great concentration to mimic their movements.

*Theseus* (v.o.) "A tedious brief scene of young Pyramus
And his love Thisby; very tragical mirth."

⌒ QUINCE works on his prologue, writes, scratches out, writes. SNOUT runs his lines.

# FORMAL GARDEN

*Evening* ⌒ To the lovers.

*Theseus*  Merry and tragical? Tedious and brief?
That is, hot ice and wondrous strange snow.

⌒ And, because he's the Duke, everyone laughs. He looks at PHILOSTRATE who smiles like a nervous rat.

*Theseus*  What are they that do play it?

# HOLDING AREA

⌒ The MECHANICALS sit on a bench, waiting, sweating, success or failure? Acceptance or rejection?

*Philostrate* (v.o.)  Hard-handed men, that work in Athens here,
Which never labored in their minds till now.

⌒ BOTTOM does his facial stretches "moa, moa." SNOUT runs his lines even faster.

*Philostrate* (v.o.)  And now have toiled
    their unbreathed memories
With the same play, against your nuptial.

*Theseus* (v.o.)  We will hear it.

⟶ A door opens—an OFFICIAL from the
palace. MASTER ANTONIO starts forward. The
OFFICIAL shakes his head, it's QUINCE he wants.
PETER QUINCE.

*Philostrate* (v.o.)  No, my noble lord.

# FORMAL GARDEN

*Night* ⟶ PHILOSTRATE is pleading.

*Philostrate*  I have heard it over,
And it is nothing, nothing in the world.

*Theseus*  I will hear that play.

# HOLDING AREA

⟶ QUINCE, the color drained from his
face, walks back into the room, takes his place
on the bench. He speaks very quietly.

*Quince*  The short and long of it is, our
    play is preferred.

⟶ Fear passes through them like a cold
wind. The running of SNOUT's lines goes into
overdrive. THISBY/FLUTE faints. BOTTOM grabs
SNUG by the collar as he tries to bolt.

# THEATER

*Night* ⟶ The seats are full aside from
the Ducal box.

# BACKSTAGE

⟶ Each of the actors in their own little
terrors. SNUG, who peeks through the curtains,
suddenly turns, points, unable to speak.

# THEATER

⟶ All rise and applaud as THESEUS and
HIPPOLYTA and the lovers take their places on a
central dais.

*Theseus* (v.o.)  . . . For never anything can
    be amiss,
When simpleness and duty tender it.
Go, bring them in.

⟶ This to catatonic PHILOSTRATE.

*Theseus*  Take your places, ladies.

*Hippolyta* (referring to Philostrate)  He says
    they can do nothing in this kind.

*Theseus*  The kinder we, to give them
    thanks for nothing.

# BACKSTAGE

⟶ QUINCE is high on a ladder next to a
shuttered window. STARVELING stands below

him. At the right moment STARVELING's job will be to open the shutters, revealing . . .

**Quince** Moonshine.

⟿ STARVELING nods. PHILOSTRATE comes backstage. "One minute."

# DAIS

⟿ PHILOSTRATE returns to the dais now almost in tears.

**Philostrate** So please Your Grace the
  Prologue is addressed.

**Theseus** Let him approach.

# STAGE

⟿ The curtain comes up, revealing the actors, the very nervous actors. SNOUT mumbles his lines like one possessed. STARVELING, in true Italian fashion, unconsciously scratches his balls. PETER QUINCE steps forward.

**Quince** Gentles, perchance you wonder at
  this show;
But wonder on, till truth make all things plain.
This man is Pyramus, if you would know;
This beauteous lady Thisby is certain.

⟿ BOTTOM clanks forward in armor fashioned from SNOUT's tinker's cart. He lifts the visor on his helmet. It falls immediately. He holds it up. THISBY/FLUTE accompanies him with surprising grace.

**Quince** This man, with lime and rough-
  cast, doth present

Wall, that vile Wall which did these lovers
  sunder.

⟿ SNOUT comes forward.

**Quince** And through Wall's chink . . .

⟿ SNOUT freezes.

**Quince** And through Wall's chink . . .

⟿ SNOUT's arm shoots up like it's spring-loaded. He makes a circle with his fingers.

**Quince** . . . poor souls, they are content
To whisper. At the which let no man wonder.
This grisly beast, which Lion hight by name,
The trusty Thisby, coming first by night,
Did scare away, or rather did affright.

⟿ SNUG attacks weakly, and THISBY/FLUTE, with a big dumb-show style gesture, flees.

QUINCE looks up to see:

# DAIS

⟿ PHILOSTRATE, from behind the DUKE, signaling him to pick up the pace.

# STAGE

⟿ QUINCE begins to run through the lines so fast, the actors can barely keep up.

**Quince** And, as she fled, her mantle she
  did fall,
Which Lion vile with bloody mouth did stain.
Anon comes Pyramus, sweet youth and tall,
And finds his trusty Thisby's mantle slain:

Whereat, with blade, with bloody blameful
blade,
He bravely broached his boiling bloody
breast.

⟿ BOTTOM glares. He wanted to make a
"moment" of this. QUINCE goes on.

*Quince* And Thisby, tarrying in mulberry
shade,
His dagger drew, and died.

⟿ Bang, he's down. The rest QUINCE
delivers as he picks up props, pulls actors to
their feet, and hurries them into the wings.

*Quince* For all the rest,
Let Lion, Moonshine, Wall, and lovers twain
At large discourse . . .

⟿ He grabs WALL, puts him in his place.

*Quince* . . . while here they do remain.

⟿ Quiet. Anticipation. QUINCE sits on
his prompt stool and waits. SNOUT stands
stock-still in the middle of the stage like . . .
well, like a wall.

# DAIS

⟿ PHILOSTRATE bites a fingernail. Pause,
pause, pause.

# STAGE

⟿ Suddenly WALL/SNOUT takes a deep
breath. The lines come out like machine-
gun fire.

*Snout* In this same interlude it doth befall
That I, one Snout by name, present a wall;
And such a wall, as I would have you think,
That had in it a crannied hole or chink.

⟿ The arm flies up. The chink appears.
BOTTOM and QUINCE exchange a hopeful
glance.

*Snout* Through which the lovers—

⟿ The barrage stops short.

*Snout* Through which the lovers—

*Quince* (*whispers*) Pyramus and Thisby.

⟿ Nothing.

*Quince* (*louder*) Pyramus and Thisby.

⟿ The lovers lean forward. The audience
leans forward. The actors lean forward.

*Quince* PYRAMUS AND THISBY!!

*Snout* (*kick-started*) . . . Pyramus and Thisby,
Did whisper often very secretly.
And this the cranny is, right and sinister,
Through which the fearful lovers are to . . .

⟿ A pause. Longer. SAY IT!

*Snout* . . . whisper.

# DAIS

*Theseus* Would you desire lime and hair
to speak better?

*Demetrius* It is the wittiest partition that
ever I heard
discourse, my lord.

⟳ A clanking from onstage

*Theseus*  Pyramus draws near the wall.
  Silence!

# STAGE

⟳ BOTTOM takes a moment, lets his armor
settle. His style is grand, operatic, declamatory.
Everything is indicated.

*Bottom*  O grim-looked night! O night
  with hue so black!
O night, which ever art when day is not!
O night, O night! Alack, alack, alack.

⟳ QUINCE mouths every word.
THISBY/FLUTE works on her curtsy.

*Bottom*  I fear my Thisby's promise if
  forgot!
And thou, O wall, O sweet, O lovely wall,
That stand'st between her father's ground and
  mine!
Thou wall, O wall, O sweet and lovely wall,
Show me thy chink, to blink through with
mine eyne!

⟳ BOTTOM takes SNOUT's arm and adjusts
"the chink" to a comfortable level.

*Bottom*  Thanks, courteous wall. Jove
  shield thee well for this!
But what see I? No Thisby do I see.
O wicked wall, through whom I see no bliss!
Cursed be thy stones for thus deceiving me!

⟳ He smacks SNOUT upside the back of
his head.

# DAIS

*Theseus*  The wall, methinks, being sensi-
  ble, should curse again.

# STAGE

⟳ Hearing this, BOTTOM walks to the
apron to address the DUKE directly.

*Bottom*  No, in truth, sire, he should not.
  "Deceiving me" is Thisby's cue.
She is to enter now, and I
am to spy her through the wall.

⟳ QUINCE cringes.

# DAIS

⟳ PHILOSTRATE has the vapors. As
BOTTOM returns to his place:

# STAGE

*Bottom*  You shall see it will fall pat as I
  told you.
Yonder she comes.

⟳ THISBY/FLUTE enters. It is surprisingly
graceful. She executes a perfect curtsy and
speaks as convincingly as her text allows.

*Flute*  O wall, full often hast thou heard
  my moans,
For parting my fair Pyramus and me!
My cherry lips have often kissed thy stones,

Lysander and
Hermia, now
husband and
wife, enjoy the
Mechanicals'
performance.

Thy stones with lime and hair knit up in thee.

*Bottom* I see a voice: now will I to the chink
To spy an I can hear my Thisby's face.
Thisby!

⟶ FLUTE looks at QUINCE. "Is that the line?
Is that the cue?"

*Bottom* Thisby!

*Flute* (*shakily*) My love thou art, my love
    . . . I think.

*Bottom* Think what thou wilt, I am thy
    lover's grace;
And, like Limander, am I trusty still.

*Flute* And I like Helen, till the Fates me
    kill.

*Bottom* O kiss me through the hole of
    this vile wall!

⟶ They approach the chink. It's an awkward piece of blocking.

*Flute* I kiss the wall's hole, not your lips at
    all.

⟶ The audience roars at this.

*Bottom* Wilt thou at Ninny's tomb—

*Quince* (o.s.) NINUS'!!

*Bottom* —meet me straightway?

*Flute* 'Tide life, 'tide death, I come
    without delay.

⟶ She curtsies to the dais and exits.
BOTTOM mounts an imaginary steed and
gallops off stage left. He gives QUINCE thumbs
up as he rides by.

**Snout** Thus have I, Wall, my part discharged so;
And, being done, thus wall away doth go.

⤳ And exits.

## BACKSTAGE

⤳ SNUG is literally clinging to the curtains
like a frightened cat. BOTTOM tries to pry him
loose.

## DAIS

*Theseus* Here come two noble beasts in,
a man and a lion.

## STAGE

⤳ BOTTOM marches out pulling behind
him a strange contraption—a wooden lion,
set on four wooden wheels. He gives it a push
and it begins to roll downstage. It picks up
speed, and it is only at the last moment that
BOTTOM grabs its leather tail to prevent it
from falling into the pit. As BOTTOM exits . . .

*Snug* You, ladies, you, whose gentle hearts
do fear
The smallest monstrous mouse that creeps on
floor,
May now perchance both quake and tremble
here,
When lion rough in wildest rage doth roar.

⤳ The tiniest of roars.

## DAIS

⤳ The faces of HERMIA and HELENA tell us
how charming it is.

## STAGE

⤳ A very human arm emerges from the
lion's side, reaches up, and lifts the lion's
wooden face like a visor to reveal SNUG.

*Snug* Then know that I, as Snug the
joiner, am
A lion fell, nor else no lion's dam;
For, if I should as lion come in strife
Into this place, 'twere pity on my life.

⤳ QUINCE emerges from the wings, and
drags the thing—SNUG and all—offstage.

## DAIS

⤳ The lovers join in.

*Theseus*
A very gentle beast, and of a good con-
science.

## BACKSTAGE

⤳ QUINCE applauds too. Things are
taking a turn for the better. Now for . . .

*Quince* Moonshine!

⌐ He signals old STARVELING to open the shutters. He does and reveals a real window sash and sill with nothing but a stone wall behind it. It is a dummy window. QUINCE pales—no moonshine. How can he have the lovers' last night without moonshine?

Moments later:

# STAGE

⌐ SNUG, still alone on the stage, roars. He pulls a pocket watch from under his lion's skin. Roars again. He looks off to see old STARVELING entering in his street clothes. He carries a lantern on a stick.

*Starveling*  This lanthorn doth the
    horned moon present—

⌐ A big laugh interrupts him. He holds up his hand.

*Starveling*  This lanthorn doth the
    horned moon present;
Myself the man i' th' moon do seem to be.

# DAIS

⌐ HIPPOLYTA snuggles up to THESEUS. She is ready for the next phase of the night's entertainment.

*Hippolyta* (a little loud)  I am aweary of
    this moon. Would he would change!

# STAGE

⌐ STARVELING, unapologetic, addresses the dais.

*Starveling*  All that I have to say is to
    tell you that
the lanthorn is the moon; I, the man i' th' moon;
this thorn bush, my thorn bush.

⌐ A sound. The click, click, click of little claws. The ratty terrier has taken this moment to make an entrance.

*Starveling*  And this dog, my dog.

⌐ The dog sits beside his old master. More laughter from the dais.

*Helena*  Silence! Here comes Thisby.

⌐ Enter. Curtsy. Speak.

*Flute*  Where is my love?

⌐ SNUG, lying in wait, lets loose a pallid roar. THISBY/FLUTE has been lying in wait too, for this "moment." She lets out a bloodcurdling scream. SNUG screams too. STARVELING drops the lantern. The dog barks.

THISBY/FLUTE flees, careful to leave her mantle behind. SNUG wools it around and exits in the other direction.

# DAIS

*Hermia*  Well roared, Lion.

*Helena*  Well run, Thisby.

*Hippolyta*  Well shone, Moon.

*Theseus*  And then came Pyramus.

# STAGE

⟶ And come he does, clanking and galloping. He dismounts, tethers his imaginary horse, hands STARVELING his lantern and moves center.

*Bottom*  Sweet Moon, I thank thee for thy
    sunny beams;
I thank thee, Moon, for shining now so bright;
For, by thy gracious, golden, glittering gleams,
I trust to take of truest Thisby sight.
But stay, O spite!
But mark, poor knight,
What dreadful dole is here!

⟶ He points emphatically to
THISBY/FLUTE's discarded shawl.

*Bottom*  Eyes, do you see?
How can it be?
O dainty duck! O dear!
Thy mantle good,
What, stained with blood!

⟶ He picks it up and immediately feels strange resistance. STARVELING's dog has the other end of it in his teeth. BOTTOM struggles to stay in character as he fights to free it.

*Bottom*  Approach, ye Furies fell!
O Fates, come, come,
Cut thread and thrum.

⟶ The dog is sailing around on the end of the scarf like an angry game fish. The fight intensifies.

*Bottom*  QUAIL . . . CRUSH . . .
CONCLUDE . . .

# DAIS

*Hippolyta*  Beshrew my heart, but I pity
the man.

# STAGE

*Bottom*  . . . and QUELLLL!

⟶ A great whiplike action. The dog loses its grip and goes sailing into the audience. Old STARVELING peers over the footlights, trying to locate it.

*Bottom*  O wherefore, Nature, didst thou
    lions frame?
Since lion vile hath here deflow'red my dear.

*Quince*  DEVOURED!

⟶ BOTTOM stops dead.

# DAIS AND BACKSTAGE

⟶ PHILOSTRATE begins a letter of resignation.

# STAGE

*Bottom*  Which is—no, no—which was
    the fairest dame
That lived, that loved, that liked, that looked
    with cheer.

Come, tears, confound;
Out, sword, and wound
The pap of Pyramus;
Ay, that left pap,
Where heart doth hop.
Thus die I.

⟶ He lifts his sword. The stab is big, violent, almost convincing.

*Bottom*  Thus, thus, thus.

⟶ With each thrust, the pained reaction of one of his fellow actors—SNOUT, QUINCE, FLUTE. He falls. There is applause for the sheer boldness of it. PETER QUINCE applauds loudest of all. BOTTOM stops it by pulling himself up on one arm.

*Bottom*  Now am I dead.

⟶ QUINCE looks befuddled at his prompt book. This is pure BOTTOM.

*Bottom*  Now am I fled;
My soul is in the sky.
Tongue, lose thy light;
Moon, take thy flight.

⟶ The old man just stands there.

*Bottom*  Moon, take thy flight.

⟶ STARVELING shuffles off. BOTTOM rises. He will use every inch of the stage.

*Bottom*  Now die,
die,
die . . .

⟶ He falls but rises again.

*Bottom*   . . . die.

⟶ Silence. THISBY/FLUTE enters. After the requisite curtsy:

*Flute*  Asleep, my love?
What, dead, my dove?

⟶ She kneels beside him.

*Flute*  O Pyramus, arise!
Speak, speak. Quite dumb?
Dead, dead?

⟶ Real tears come to her eyes, a real performance.

*Flute*  A tomb
Must cover these lily lips,
This cherry nose,
These yellow cowslip cheeks,
Are gone, are gone.

# DAIS

⟶ The lovers no longer laughing.

# STAGE AND BACKSTAGE

*Flute*  His eyes were green as leeks.
O Sisters Three,
Come, come to me,
With hands as pale as milk;
Lay them in gore,
Since you have shore
With shears his thread of silk.

⟶ QUINCE is weeping. So is SNUG.

*Flute*  Tongue, not a word.

Come, trusty sword,
Come, blade, my breast imbrue!

## DAIS

→ HIPPOLYTA, enrapted, mouths the word "No."

## STAGE

→ THISBY/FLUTE stabs herself painfully, convincingly.

*Flute*  And, farewell, friends.
Thus Thisby ends.
Adieu, adieu, adieu.

→ She wilts like a flower—a silence, a long silence. Then big heartfelt applause. Against impossible odds, a star is born. BOTTOM, even though this is the ovation he dreamed of for himself, stands and joins in. THISBY/FLUTE is overcome.

## DAIS

→ THESEUS wipes away a surreptitious tear.

*Theseus*  Moonshine and Lion are left to bury the dead.

*Demetrius* (equally moved)  Ay, and Wall too.

*Bottom,
Snout, and
Flute
perform
for the Duke
and Duchess.*

# STAGE

As the company assembles for a bow, BOTTOM shouts over the applause, very familiar now with the DUKE.

*Bottom*  No, I assure you; the wall is
    down that parted their fathers.
Will it please you to see
the epilogue, or to hear a Bergomask dance
between two of our company?

# DAIS

*Theseus*  No epilogue, I pray you; for
    your play needs no excuse.
Never excuse, for when the players are
all dead, there need none to be blamed.

# STAGE

The MECHANICALS look at each other, not quite certain how to take this. They bow and exit the stage.

# BACKSTAGE

The MECHANICALS wait nervously in the wings.

# DAIS

THESEUS writes something on a piece of paper. Hands it to PHILOSTRATE.

# BACKSTAGE

Silence as PHILOSTRATE appears. He gives the paper to QUINCE. He opens it, reads:

*Quince*  "Very notably discharged."

A wave of relief, a little bit of dignity. QUINCE presents the certificate to BOTTOM, who looks at it for a moment and shakes his head. He walks to THISBY/FLUTE and gives it to him.

# STAIRCASE

*Night*  A remarkable circular frescoed staircase. THESEUS, HIPPOLYTA, and the lovers reach the top.

*Theseus*  The iron tongue of midnight
    hath told twelve.
Lovers, to bed; 'tis almost fairy time.

One can feel the anticipation of the wedding night to come. They say their farewells and head toward their several chambers.

*Theseus*  A fortnight hold we this solemnity,
In nightly revels and new jollity.

Below, the servants extinguish the lights. Again nothing but night and silence. A pause, then the area at the top of the stairs begins to glow. In that light appear TITANIA and OBERON. And below begin to assemble a host of little firefly creatures, little pricks of light moving in the dark house. And in every nitch and cranny a fairy nymph or satyr. OBERON holds his love's hand, addresses his glimmering subjects.

*Oberon* Now, until the break of day,
Through this house each fairy stray.

# CORRIDOR

⌒ PUCK rides grinning down the wide hallway on his bicycle. He lets a stream of little firelight fairies trail from his saddlebag.

*Oberon* (*v.o.*) To the best bride-bed will we,
Which by us shall blessed be.

# LYSANDER & HERMIA'S CHAMBER

⌒ LYSANDER and HERMIA make gentle love. Suddenly they find themselves bathed in an almost holy glow.

*Oberon* (*v.o.*) And the issue there create
Ever shall be fortunate.

⌒ They see the room full of such a miraculous host of fireflies.

# DEMETRIUS & HELENA'S CHAMBER

⌒ DEMETRIUS holds HELENA close to him as they watch from their bed the magical dance of light.

*Oberon* (*v.o.*) So shall all the couples three
Ever true in loving be.

# GRAND STAIRCASE

⌒ OBERON is arm in arm with TITANIA. The CHANGELING BOY stands between them.

*Oberon* Trip away; make no stay;
Meet me all by break of day.

⌒ With a great sweep of his arm, he creates from the rest of his fire fairy subjects, a glowing whirlwind that rises up and explodes like a firework. When the shower of sparks fall, the chamber is empty.

# PIAZZA

*Night* ⌒ QUINCE, BOTTOM, FLUTE, et al. have reached the well in the center of the square. They say their farewells, big Italian embraces. We hear the phrase "most notably discharged." They go their ways, leaving the Piazza empty except for an old street sweeper. He stops working, takes off his hat. It is PUCK. He speaks directly to camera:

*Puck* If we shadows have offended,
Think but this, and all is mended.

⌒ Cut to:

# FARMHOUSE

*Night* — The old enchanted FORE-MAN suddenly sits up, sweating in his bed.

*Puck* (v.o.) That you have but slumb'red here,
While these visions did appear.

— He feels his face—still the orange and yellow cap but no bristles, no snout.

*Puck* (v.o.) And this weak and idle theme,
No more yielding but a dream.

— He looks at the stuffed boar's head that stares back at him from the wall.

# PIAZZA

*Night* — PUCK pulls himself up to sit on the well.

*Puck* Gentles, do not reprehend:
If you pardon, we will mend.
Else the Puck a liar call.

— He points up to a window.

Cut to:

# BOTTOM'S BEDROOM

*Night* — BOTTOM slowly puts away his white suit. His WIFE appears at the turn, grunts in contempt at his delusions of grandeur. He shrugs. She walks away. Alone now, he hangs his trousers, careful to

*Lysander and Hermia awake from their wedding-night slumber.*

keep the crease. He feels something in the pocket. It is the little fairy crown from the woods. He turns it over in his hand, a strange little trinket.

He blows out his light and goes to his window. One last look at the moon. He sighs. All very strange.

But before he turns away, something catches his eye; a light that flits and flies and dances outside his window. As he looks at it, it expands and takes on a form—of TITANIA, his fairy love, suspended in the air before him. They look at each other with great curiosity. She reaches out her hand and touches the windowpane. He opens it. Then reaching for his hand, she takes the crown and slips it onto his finger, like a wedding ring. She smiles a little sadly, fades, and is gone. BOTTOM is left smiling too. His eyes fill up with a strange kind of joy.

## PIAZZA

*Night* — PUCK shrugs—"not so bad"—and hops down from the well.

*Puck* So, good night unto you all.
Give me your hands, if we be friends,
And Robin shall restore amends.

— With that he throws the broom over his shoulder and walks away—just an ordinary goblin in a little Tuscan town, on a midsummer's eve, his little form an ever-diminishing silhouette against the full white disk of the moon.